THE
NEO-DECADENT
COOKBOOK

Edited by

Brendan Connell and Justin Isis

The Neo-Decadent Cookbook
edited by Brendan Connell and Justin Isis
ISBN: 978-1-908125-97-2

Cover Art by David Rix

Publication Date: August 2020

CONTENTS

7 - Manifesto of Neo-Decadent Cooking - Brendan Connell and Justin Isis

11 - The Bias of Affinity - Ross Scott-Buccleuch

15 - London in Three Courses: First Course - David Rix

23 - The Mushroom Omelette - Catherine Dousteyssier-Khoze

27 - The Devil's Alchemist - Jason Rolfe

35 - Koliva - Daniel Corrick

47 - Household Hints - Brendan Connell

51 - Cooking Australia - Colby Smith

55 - Heavenly Victuals - Jessica Sequeira

59 - The Vertical Table - Justin Isis

67 - London in Three Courses: Second Course - David Rix

75 - Some Necessary Words on the Subject of Fruit - Quentin S. Crisp

83 - The Immaculate Scrambled Automat - Damian Murphy

93 - Revolt of the Kitchens - Jessica Sequeira

103 - The Wild Hunt - Douglas Thompson

109 - Machines that Eat Flowers - Justin Isis

117 - Seeds - Ursula Pflug

125 - The Night-Drinkers - Jason Rolfe

133 - Insalata di parole - Brendan Connell

137 - A Food Critic's Nightmare - Jessica Sequeira

141 - London in Three Courses: Third Course - David Rix

149 - My Dream Vacation - Lawrence Burton

155 - Nettle Tea - Ursula Pflug

157 - The Enteric Universe - Justin Isis

163 - About the Authors

MANIFESTO OF NEO-DECADENT COOKING

Brendan Connell and Justin Isis

1. In past ages, the primary purpose of food was to fortify the body and to bring the spirit in closer contact with the gods. Today, however, through the decayed state of the social structure, its primary purpose, among all who are not starving, is to entertain and to declaim one's STATUS and to display a flaccid costume of COMMUNITY. The Neo-Decadents, instead of rejecting this sorry state, embrace it, shouting loudly from the cafés and rooftops to the crowded boulevards, summoning both the curious and the confounded.

2. Some exist on diets of cartilage, worms, or fried brains, while others sip dew from flowers and turn away from rancid flesh with disgust.

All embracing, however, we are able to see the ULTIMATE in countless actions. We simply DEMAND WAKEFULNESS.

3. To eat is to kill. MURDERERS EVERY-WHERE! We see them lunging at us, their lips wet with hunger, their eyes sharp with lust. Ever-abundant, we let them dine on us, on our sinews and ideas, on the music of our mouths and the smell of our loins.

4. Cooking must be taken outside the confines of the material world. The MIGHTY FRUIT is whipped up from ideas, from savage nightmares and whispering dreams. Recipes must be SHOCKING, and wine glasses full of the sweet blood of angels. Dining on over-exposed ragues and phosphorescent pies, in which rest unnamable meats and bizarre sinews, TRUE UNDERSTANDING AND SCIENCE EXPLODE!

5. Have you ever sautéed geometrical sex or eaten fate from the breasts of Minerva?

AWAY WITH DISCRETION! The mirrors and crystals reflect tastes, the curtains are replete with rare pungencies. . . . MODERN COOKING MUST BE DESTROYED! WE WILL NEVER EAT FROM GIANT WHITE PLATES!

6. The enteric nervous system—the true seat of the soul—demands an appropriately slavering ministry. From the ENTERIC PULPIT we proclaim the need for recombinant recipes, aleatoric cooking. Rock salt rubbed on dripping flanks. Tapioca teas and spider cereal for newborn sorcerers.

7. NO MORE NUTRITIOUS SLIMES BLENDED AND CANNED! We dream of fruit-meats, candied vegetables, luminous vitamin-and-mineral ice. The utensil-claws of the future rending fleshy portals in the merely POSSIBLE.

8. RATS, CROWS AND COCKROACHES: true gourmands of the urban buffet. We leave

the restaurants to them, taking our appetites elsewhere. The raw planes and angles of industrial coffins and financial towers will be converted into enormous picnic spreads, concrete tables laden with delicacies. When the electricity fails, it will be time for sentimental desserts: winter melons and youthful ambitions roasted in moonlight. We will PURGE OURSELVES OF MERE PHYSICAL HUNGER AND DINE IN THE LAPS OF IMPROVISED GODS.

THE BIAS OF AFFINITY

Ross Scott-Buccleuch

Begin only with aperitifs of murderous fervour,
for the burgeoning of gustation post-multicide
blooms, flourishes, OUTLASTS.

sour acceptance
acquired
*   (although gagging)*

Abhor the finitude of the menu.
Force addendums, collaboration,
INTERFERENCE.

Oh voluptuous papillae
and vagus villainy!

within
* anterior tongue*

within
> *artificial surface*

within
EROS
> *without* /end

The hand compromises the tongue:
uncharted gustations lie beyond their
sundering.

e r u p t i o n s   *after decreased*
                            access to MEAT

Abandon dislikes on a whim, like a sudden
avulsion or apostasy.

diffusion of medulla
> *cream associated autonomic*
gene sequence
> *across salad component*

The ingredient is an impediment!
Release the repast from the confines of the
recipe!

peristalsis is conformity
DISAVOW

liberated from i n g e s t i o n
                    consequence of residual
SWEET response

Capacitant, seeker of apogee.

suggesting:
do and *only* INTERACT

Usurp the tongue as arbiter of *choice*:
overrule distaste and
IGNORE the bias of affinity.

LONDON IN THREE COURSES: FIRST COURSE

David Rix

If you spend any amount of time in London, you will eventually meet an elephant.

Off the top of my head and with no immediate research, I can remember one standing on Camden High Street Bridge—another sitting on the church wall at Shoreditch, one somewhere on the south bank, one near Brick Lane, one under the East Cross roadbridge where my narrowboat the Eibonvale was currently moored—others as well, though I am hazy as to the locations. All carved of quiet stone and firmly, professionally installed—yet somehow subversive. Unofficial.

And I, at least, have no idea who the Elephant Man is.

On that day, I was poking around on Hackney Marsh, looking for the ingredients for some of the one hundred and twenty six Hackney Liqueurs (at least, as I had slowly catalogued them over the years). I had found a few: . . . #8 (elderflower), #20 (wild rose), #76 (hogweed) and #42 (fresh marsh reedstem) and I was getting impatient. On a quest for some #62 (lime blossom), I pushed further into the woods, leaving the paths behind me—always risky. The undergrowth was assaulting my skin—tormenting me with nettles (#38) and hawthorn (#14, berries—and #92. blossoms). It was a trammelled reminder of wilderness, here bounded by the colourful Lee and the grey city beyond.

I stumbled through the nettle beds until I came upon what I initially took to be a deadfall—except that it was arranged in an unnatural ring shape. Obscure though it was, and almost buried in the foliage though it was, it had to be man-made.

I stumbled through it, my feet sinking painfully among the branches—but in the clearing in the centre something very mysterious. A tall birch tree stump projected above the seemingly virgin nettles—and perched on it, an elephant. An unfinished elephant, its lines only roughly hewn in soft stone. I stared round the woods—and suddenly #62 didn't seem so important. I could see no signs of any of the trails—no signs of human disturbance. Yet here was the elephant. A new creation intended for some obscure wall or pillar in the city? Manufactured here surrounded by green? After a few moments staring in amazement, I made my way back out over that deadfall, my skin prickling.

Arriving at the East Cross Road Bridge. My old seventy-foot narrowboat, the Eibonvale, was moored just a few metres down, but instead I made my way to the small camp nestled safely in the shelter of the concrete. There was a scent of food in the air—something that probably had wings roasting by the fire.

"Hello, Liqueur Man." A familiar voice.

I glanced round and Lauren latched on with a rib-bending hug. She was quite short, but solid and strong, her hair dyed in ragged streaks of dark and light, her clothes mostly black but with splashes of sharp-coloured ornamentation.

"Haven't seen you around for a while," I said.

"Oh you know me. I always miss looking after this place."

I glanced round with a warm feeling at the cluttered world beneath the bridge. Wild and deeply unofficial—a tangle that hazed from utilitarian campsite to workshop to studio to art gallery, all illuminated in the firelight. Big, complex constructions reached up towards the road deck—lavish colourful spraypaint on the pillars and walls. Including the elephant, of course. Two-foot high and mounted on a rough wooden pedestal. And the boats moored here were simultaneously some of the most untidy and the most intriguing in East London.

"Besides," she said, "I need a spraycan in my hand again. It's no fun out of town."

Lauren accompanied me through the sculpture garden to where the still stood against the rearing concrete. It was a fine device, with a lot of pipes gleaming copper-dark in the firelight. I grabbed a carboy and she helped me decant clear spirit. Then we lugged it to the Eibonvale.

"I double-moored you," Lauren said. I smiled at the familiar sight of her boat, the lavishly graffiti-covered Wandering Eye, nestling comfortably up against mine. It blazed with art if anything even more than I remembered—art that she herself and various friends had contributed at one point or another. Everybody shared. That was how street art worked—even on boats.

We stepped down into the narrow but cosy interior of the Eibonvale—a space filled with bottles on every available shelf. Enough liqueurs and bitters for all the London canals. Without even asking, I poured out two glasses of the last and latest liqueur on my list (#126—mallow seed) and handed one to her.

"Welcome back," I said, and she responded with a happy nod.

"I think we should leave these two boats tied together for a while," she said.

I smiled and nodded. The Wandering Eye and the Eibonvale fit together rather well, I always felt.

Then we quickly set to work tidying, washing and cutting the various ingredients I had found—filling bottles. They would steep for varying numbers of weeks before being strained and sealed to age. Half a year hence, it would be these that were handed around as the fire blazed beneath the concrete bridge.

Then finally it was time to join the others and relax. And yes, what was roasting had wings—some of it anyway. But there was more. There was something long and thin coiled around a stick. Snake. No doubt one of the pythons that live wild here. Served with roasted parakeet and suitably detoxed pigeon, it would be a welcome meat feast on a cold spring night in the waterworld. To that, I added a salad of ground ivy and cooked hogweed shoots. As well as a bottle of #2 (sloe).

"Did you know the Elephant Man does his work in our woods?" I asked, a few minutes later.

"Yes," she said. "Among other places, or so they say."

I raised my eyebrows, mildly surprised that she knew. I had been in and around the East End and the marshes for years, but had never known this. That was how London worked, however. It was too big for any one mind to encompass.

"You ever see him?"

She shook her head, then stared off into the dark to where our own elephant stood quietly. "I always wondered if he is actually real . . ."

The doom came at dawn. It woke me up with a nasty jolt—shouting voices. Fluorescent jackets. And my heart sank.

From the safety of the Eibonvale, I watched as the camp was dismantled—a frantic battleground of activity as people tried to get the sculptures to safety before they could be loaded onto a refuse truck. The tents were in ruins. Lauren was in the crowd and I watched as she wrestled a small figure out of the hands of one of the workers and came running in the direction of the Eibonvale. She came crashing down the stairs, tears streaming down her face. I stared at her for a moment then closed my eyes, feeling a dull rage that was all too familiar.

I ducked into the Eibonvale's tiny bathroom and unhooked the mirror from the wall, then stepped ashore. Holding the mirror against my chest, facing forward, I marched into the centre of the camp, stepping over the debris and destroyed tents.

"Excuse me," I said. The fluorescent jacket turned sharply, stared at himself in the mirror for a second, then blinked and retreated a few steps. I quietly picked up the elephant sculpture that he had been removing and carried it back on-board. I set it carefully on a shelf, then returned to the rear deck. But there wasn't much else to salvage by this time. With astonishing speed, it was all over—everything removable was gone, and everything fixed or painted on the concrete columns was a lost cause. Soon, no doubt, to be painted over with random blocks of white paint. The space under the East Cross bridge had become a wasteland.

Lauren joined me, her face still soaked. "I seem to be out of a job," she muttered, her shaking voice negating the dryness of her words. "What is there for me with no sculpture garden to watch over?" She sat on my sofa and stared out of the window, eyes dull. Stared first at the demolished camp, then in the other direction, at the low-rise Hackney Wick housing estate across the water, where people lived much greyer lives.

THE MUSHROOM OMELETTE

Catherine Dousteyssier-Khoze

This is an old family recipe, with a personal tweak or two. It is versatile and, I think, very tasty. It certainly elevates the humble omelette to new, dizzying heights. No one who's ever tried it has found fault with it, that I know of.

Needless to say, the ingredients, eggs and mushrooms alike, must be impeccably fresh. The putrescent or *faisandé*, as the French say, has no place here. This is neither a recipe for hare stew nor *civet de lièvre à l'ancienne*, nor some misplaced cultural ravings on the virtues of Icelandic hákarl (yes, *that* fermented shark treat).

You will need peacock eggs. Five or six should suffice, for up to four people. I usually make this omelette for one or two carefully handpicked guests. If you do not have access to peacock eggs, which would be regrettable, I am unsure what to advise. Nothing can quite replace them. It has something to do with that unique gamey tang. Perhaps you could attempt to procure flamingo eggs. But I'm afraid that I'm letting my love of bold colours and semi-exotic birds speak here, I have never tried such eggs, whose yolk, by the way, is yellow, not pink.

Where was I? Peacock eggs. As soon as you are back from the forest with your basket of mushroom goodies, go harvest the eggs. Don't forget to close the peacock pen behind you— peacocks are dreadfully aggressive birds—and repair to your kitchen den where you can treat yourself to a restorative drink (avoid yolk-based cocktails). If you are in a playful and munificent mood—and why shouldn't you be if you stumbled earlier on a patch of dapperling lepiotas in your favourite wood?—you can indulge in a spot of table decorating. Bring out the family silverware and your mother's precious Lalique vase—the grand one with Bacchantes. Place the iridescent peacock feathers you've just fought for in the vase as a centrepiece.

I don't have much to say on the subject of the mushrooms themselves.

Just cook the dapperling lepiotas, also known as *lepiota brunneoincarnata*, any way you fancy. Darling dapperlings. Dapper little caplings! Don't they sparkle, don't they shine, the still dewy precious things! With their creamy pink stems and fruity odour and white, pearly gills, who could resist them?

For preparation, I usually stick to the no-nonsense advice provided by Maestro Martino in his treatise on *The Art of Cooking* (*Libro de arte coquinaria*, circa 1465):

Clean the mushrooms very well.
Let them boil in water with two or three buttons of garlic and white bread (this is done because they are poisonous by nature).
Then remove them and drain the water so that they are dry, and then fry them in good oil or lard.
And when they are cooked, place over them various spices.

Everyone's here. The time has come to whisk the eggs.

Add a few twigs of saffron—I am partial to Kashmiri saffron of the Mongra grade. I know, pure extravagance. But you must send your guests off in style—it's the very least you can do.

Things may become a bit hazy during the cooking process.

Quite often, I can't remember that part.

Have you brought the crusty *pain de campagne* and leftover homemade wild boar pâté to the table? You will have to make do with it yourself—you are plagued with a mushroom allergy that does not allow you to partake of the gourmet treat. In between mouthfuls of fluffy omelette, they usually agree that your condition is nothing short of tragic.

THE DEVIL'S ALCHEMIST

Jason Rolfe

"Existence is an imperfection."
—Sartre

The cellar is dark, and though blessed with sufficiently expensive waterproofing and apt drainage I can still detect the sweetly subtle sickness of wood rot, hints of dampness that tickle an allergic reaction from my nose. The absence of sunlight and the unwavering temperature make this place—our furnace room—an ideal setting for the alchemies of fermentation. I've read countless stories about brewing as a sacred act, a ritual performed by alchemists and witches in the secret corners of the darkest places. The chants and dances performed by these wondrous women were meant to draw the most suitable spirit to their shadowy casks. If the spirit was exceptional, these alchemists placed logs of spruce or birch at the bottom of their fermenting vats; the ubiquitous yeast would penetrate the wood, lusty in its search for sticky-sweet sap, making it easier for the brewer to transfer the ensnared spirit from one fermentation vat to another. It was common, so I've read, for a mother to give a log, pregnant with the family's strain of yeast, to her daughter as a wedding gift. This was not a tradition adhered to by my mother-in-law. She gave us the gift of money; money and a countertop convection oven, its façade as steel and stainless as our microwave. So here I am, not far removed from that small appliance or the dawn of the twenty-first century, rediscovering my alchemical roots—roots so recently uncovered by a popular genealogy website and the associated DNA test that traced my storied lineage from suburban Toronto to the time-distant wilds of Abyssinia.

I lost interest in my job fourteen months ago. It would be self-satisfying to walk away from it, to lose myself in my books and vinyl records, but this city isn't for the feint of wallet, and while my wife's income is respectable, it's not enough to cover the cost of life.

"Death," she once said, wrapped as she was in Melancholy's monstrous arms, "would be far more economically viable." Our savings began bleeding the moment we bought this house, and despite severing ties with the local telecom, our second car, and the coffee shop we used to frequent on a nightly basis, we've yet to stay its scarlet flow. We've been drowning, and while we can see the diffused sunlight overhead, the tangled weeds of liability hold us just beneath the surface. The brackish water of unpaid bills is quickly displacing the air of middle-class life within our lungs. I've stopped buying vinyl, old blues records that scratch out the devil-bound legacies of men like Robert Johnson and Honeyboy Edwards. The imperfect beauty of those flawed recordings has filled my soul with joyful sadness for thirty years. Before selling the carefully curated collection, I've begun another project; a new hobby I hope will prove the salvation of those coveted disks. I've begun brewing mead.

Although indirectly related to the matter at hand, it should be noted that Honeyboy was with Robert Johnson the night he was poisoned. It's relevant in that while most believe the whiskey Johnson drank was laced with strychnine, Honeyboy always disputed that particular notion. Like Honeyboy, the toxicology textbooks I've read suggest that strychnine's appalling taste could not have been disguised by whiskey. It would have taken something sweeter, less familiar to the Bluesman's tongue. So there it is—the incidental link between Robert Johnson's death and my new hobby—a scratch that cuts across two otherwise unrelated tracks.

When the record skips, you simply lift the needle, place it back down and move on.

All yeasts are unique, judiciously chosen and lovingly raised for their inimitable flavours and style. They persist, having passed from vat to vat, from shaman to medicine woman, alchemist to witch, brewer to brewer through fading millennia to this day. The strains linger in perpetuity, floating like ageless angels, descending from above to bless our meads with their divine kiss. Mead has been called by many different names in a myriad of places along history's storied path. To my long-distant Abyssinian ancestors it was *t'ej*, fermented manna made from the twigs and leaves of *Rhamnus prinoides*. Like other traditional meads, *t'ej* distinguishes itself by the addition of organic elements. Alchemists of old used various plants to add essence to their mead—taste or tonic, curative or psychotropic—qualities that eased or afflicted the troubled, both in body and in mind. As a haven for yeast these plants hasten fermentation, or birth it in sterile mediums such as pasteurized honey, pasteurized fruit juices or refined sugar. The soul of my mead is raw honey, procured locally at a mildly outrageous price. The botanical ingredients contribute acids, tannins, nitrogen and phytochemical growth factors that stimulate the development of yeast. Because honey is nitrogen deficient, these botanical additives are an essential part of the fermentation process.

In village *t'ej* production, honey is either collected from wild nests or produced in traditional barrel-type hives, and thus contains broken combs, wax, pollen and bees. The belief persists that crude honey makes better mead than refined honey. Pollen, propolis, royal jelly, even dead bees and wax provide more diverse nutrients to sustain the fermentation. Despite its subtle hints of diesel and a misleading façade of sweetness, *t'ej* contains a high level of alcohol, depending, of course, on the length of time it spends fermenting. Mine has been hiding in the dark for each of February's 28 days. The impurities outlined above have floated to the top and can now be removed. Once refined these imperfections surrender wax, the remainder of which my ancestors referred to as *fagulo*, which they strained in a cloth and used to clean their *mitads*, the large clay disks upon which they cooked *injera*. I disregard this debris. Its purification or its later use isn't my concern and would only serve to reveal the ingredients I've used to craft this particular mead.

It took Robert Johnson three days to die. Honeyboy brought him to his mother, who stayed with him until his death. Johnson blamed the devil for his demise, begged her to take his guitar and hang it on the wall. He told her she'd been right all along—that blues was the devil's music and that Satan's hellhounds were biting at his heels. To blame the devil is to absolve ourselves of blame for the poor decisions we make. To say a man is evil for murdering another in a fit of jealous rage is irresponsible. To consider someone evil simply because they seek an escape from debt at the expense of another is pure fallacy. If I'm convinced of anything it's this: that neither good nor evil exist in this world. We are, at our very core, all animals adhering to the base philosophy that only the strong survive; not the so-called good or those considered evil, but the strong. Everything else is utterly and completely arbitrary. We're imperfect creatures living in an imperfect world. As Sartre once said, "existence is imperfect"; but like mead, it can be purified.

KOLIVA

Daniel Corrick

As Constantin ducked out of the church-porch and began his way through the baked, foul smelling streets to catch the evening tram back to his lodgings, the taste of koliva lingered in his mouth. He'd taken the brown velvety grains with their shroud-white dustings of initials with his finger-tips and eaten reverently. Now his taste-buds were coated in a moist blanket of spicy sweetness.

Constantin did not enjoy the taste of sweet food. Not for him were the syrupy pastries, candied nuts and sweetmeats of his home nation, the chocolate dainties favoured by the Germans, or the heavy puddings of the English. He satiated his appetite, in recent years almost too meagre to note, on dark bread with sour sheep's cheese, on bitter greens bearing a saint's name, and on paltry cuts of meat fried by his landlord's daughter on an oil stove. Besides the iron-tainted wine of the mountains, he drank English gin and French absinthe—spurning nativism's scented brandies and spiced liqueurs.

But he always ate koliva to remember those who had provided him with strong emotions. An atheist, he hated all forms of free-thought, Bolshevism and reformism, ideologies which would strip away the stage dressing necessary for life (by which of course he meant his life), leaving it as blank and functionally ugly as the walls of a sanatorium. The funerary dish was as much a part of this backdrop as correct neck ties, the monarch's head on coinage or the countless classical references in his poetry.

He had been consuming it frequently of late. Traditionally one partook of the sweet meal on the memorial of the dear one's passing and as part of several Lenten festivals. Constantin, a man whose character blended the sensualist's roving dissatisfaction with the introvert's abstracted rumination, had, in the course of a long life, accumulated quite a number of these memorial dates; seldom did a month go by without one of these anniversaries. He was too much the sophisticate of his time—urbane, world-weary, pleasure-seeking yet aloof; a man who gained as much satisfaction recounting infamies as indulging in them—to acknowledge values beyond the niceties of taste, and too fond of his own cynicism to acknowledge regrets.

His mouth and tongue retained their capacity for memory though, flesh memories, vivid associative afterimages, even if his mind preferred to recall these life events as nicely written episodes in the private biography of some acolyte.

He thought of Wheat, the priest at the little church where his mother took him for instruction, a vital hulking giant of a man whose hard body and tangled hair were as bleached and elemental as the exposed mountain rock. It had been he who had first shown the young Constantin the taste of passion, laying a heavy hand on the boy's shoulder and pressing his hot mouth against his when no resistance showed itself. Constantin had greedily sought out Wheat's company over the next few months; eager to discover all he could about his own body. Very quickly, though, the boy had felt a sense of sly mastery over his aged lover, who was incapable of even finding words to describe their amours, and who, though by his activities able to bridge the gap between this world and that of the *Symposium*, had certainly never read it.

Wheat had drowned soon afterwards; not crushed by roiling waves as would befit his Olympian frame, but by falling down a well in a neighbouring courtyard whilst drunk.

By then Constantin was already involved with Almond, the doctor's ward. The two, of the same age, had shared the same tutor and soon too were sharing mock-Petronian epigrams. He had loved the other boy's supple olive-tinted flesh with just the first hint of down beginning to appear on his cheeks. The two had proclaimed each other dearer than brothers and pledged eternal fealty. Almond too had departed swiftly; one day he took a cut from a boot-scraper, and by the end of the week he was abed with fever and within a month dead. Even the common decorum of a burial was denied to him, as his uncle, combing the highest philanthropic tendencies with the bitterest anti-clericalism, offered his body to the University for dissection. Constantin had borne this all dry-eyed, only able to shed a few tears years later when several of his poems dealing with the incident were published.

He lowered the brim of his hat to shield himself from the glare of the fume-coloured sky. On the pavement opposite, a man with the most disgusting little black dog was selling oranges to a stream of disgorged office boys.

There were others, less significant but still brought swimming back by the sweet flavour. Raisin, the tall sad-eyed wife of a customs officer; her seduction, if so active a term could be used for such an idle momentary appetite, had been primarily motivated by interest, akin to that of the boy who swallows a glass of spirits for the first time despite being appalled by the burning sensation, than any blood-born passion. The bodies of women always felt too animalistic and alien to Constantin. After a couple of days he scattered her letters into the fire and thought no more of it. Sesame, the pale half-Arab who lived beside his first university lodgings and had vanished at summer's end. Constantin had assuaged his grief with a pseudonymous poem about a boy whose skin browns and lips thicken with age.

A black cigarette was necessary to fortify himself for the clanking monstrosity of the tram. As he smoked, Constantin savoured the next memory; one of the lodestones of his psyche.

Honey, his Ganymede, his golden ideal. This young demi-god had been the model of a painter friend from university; the first time Constantin had seen him he'd been posing as the dying Adberus, a shining body against a blue silk screen awaiting the pitch-black mare. What divine symmetry! What perfection of limb, torso and visage! In the three years they had been lovers, Honey had been the muse and guiding light of his work, as if the Platonic sun lived within his noble flesh, radiating forth perfection and shaping every poem, every verse, every line in its unattainable image. When, as often happened in the first months of their relationship, Honey expressed desire to read these publications Constantin rebuked him sharply: "You do not try to read my poetry—you are my poetry!"

In the end it was these little impositions that begun the crack which sundered Heaven from Earth. Who was it for the beloved to interrupt the lover's contemplation of him! More than the artless hankering for art, there developed a tendency towards idle talk, petty habits picked up, arbitrary opinions and preferences wilfully upheld. It was as if the youth were seeking to sabotage his own perfection! When the time of parting came, Constantin did not mourn. What was important was not the actuality but the ideal of Honey of which he alone was custodian, an essence to be diffused and smeared over all things.

Seated on the tram, surrounded by the sweating mess of city life, Constantin picked sweet particles from his teeth and thought ruefully of how short those around him fell from any ideal.

The only artist he had come close to loving—if that was the right word to describe the cool, almost withdrawn erotic link the two shared—had been Anise, the son of a wealthy Cypriot shipping magnate and rising star of the "new poetry". Constantin had lived with him and his mistress Parsley for six years in their villa at Limassol. Anise's verse was fragmentary, modernistic, violent—dark puncture marks across the page. Unlike Constantin's "sensualist's classicism" his themes were of modernity, disorder, nihilism and the machine, the only historical allusions being the all-pervading influence of John of Revelation, the mark of a barely suppressed childhood religious neurosis.

During readings, or after particularly arduous compositions, he would become maniacal, drunk on his own work, proclaiming the ruins of the future:

> The Stars are ripened kernels
> To be ground down
> By the wings of aeroplanes

His wife Parsley watched these outbursts silently and with a permanent sphinx-like smile. She was the daughter of a Russian émigré, very beautiful but of an angular androgynous figure and detached air which put one in mind of some radiant inhuman being, a sylph or an angel. For some reason Constantin never remembered any of their conversations. An angel's forbearance was required to deal with her husband's outbursts, though. As the years passed, the fits of mania grew longer and more extreme until they were forced to keep a doctor in attendance to administer sedatives. Finally it became necessary to keep Anise confined to his room. One autumn night, from his balcony, Constantin heard his friend raving about how the stars were to fall and burn the earth. After listening in silence for hours he went to find

Parsley; she was seated by a dresser, the purple glow of dawn just strong enough to outline the contours of her ivory body. Saying nothing, he had slipped an arm around her boy-like hips and pulled her to the bed. The scent and texture of her body had been pleasingly ambiguous. Then it was all over; the next day Anise managed to stealthily kindle a fire from loose manuscripts which spread unimpeded, eventually consuming the entire villa along with its owners. Constantin had spurned funerary services in order to begin the first of his memorial sonnets.

Out on the streets again Constantin pondered the sheer banality of the *bourgeoisie*. Mothers not yet thirty with skin like old fruit rinds, pasty young men hankering after motor-cars, nondescript families, marriage certificate amorists—it was hard to imagine these beings having the same concreteness, let alone the same immortality, as that of poetry.

The festivals came and went, the koliva was consumed, the sacred memories preserved against the crudity of time. There were others; many, many others . . . Pepper, an English bank clerk ground down by officialdom and an official wife; Cinnamon with his powerful thighs; Chickpea, so wholesome yet so satisfying. But out of all those remembered only one other had approached the noble beauty of love. This individual had not been a lover in a traditional sense—Constantin had seen him but once and never lain hands on him—but he'd won a greater place in his heart and in his verse than many who surrendered to his embraces. It had been near noon on a spring day and he had been walking from a friend's villa on the outskirts of Chalandri. By the side of the road a group of three labourers had just finished breaking up the grey soil of an abandoned garden. Constantin had stopped and exchanged greetings, admiring their hard sinewy bodies and grinning faces drenched with sweat. The lads had flung their picks down and laughed, until suddenly their leader—a tall youth with clipped dark curls, an aquiline nose and thin fierce smile—had stumbled and fallen, never to rise again. As the others bent to help their fellow, Constantin took in the fallen hero's face: three seeds of dark blood ran down one cheek and his lips parted in a look of erotic supplication. A doctor said it had been a rare defect of the heart. Constantin had wept at the nobility of the sight for weeks. He'd never learnt the youth's name: instead he called him Pomegranate and celebrated his memorial with extreme punctiliousness.

Like the fading day, Constantin's pilgrimage of remembrance neared its end as he came through the narrow streets to the door of the little tobacconist shop above which he lived. He was glad to be away from people and looked forward to the evening ahead: fresh cigarettes, a pot of tea, poems to be read over in satisfaction and regret, maybe even an egg lightly done on rusk. With this hungry thought, the taste of koliva returned to him with its overwhelming sweetness. Delicate, tender, profound—how delicious these memories were! And then, as the fierce smouldering sun disappeared behind the rooftops, Constantin fell to his knees and began to vomit.

HOUSEHOLD HINTS

Brendan Connell

Meals can be colour-coded.

Keep company with those who are cheerful, those who suck on pears as if they were wounds, and who pronounce their sexual urges as if they were laws.

Supply guests with a single huge spoon each, regardless of what is being served. This is the best way to stop them from talking about their struggles during meal time.

Avoid things that are overly relaxing, such as warm rooms and soft mattresses.

One should cut bread with a knife that has been used for suicide.

Dining in a solitary hut is the summit of extravagance.

Appropriate incense should be lit to regulate the mood. The air can be cleansed by burning buttons of peyote.

For dinner parties, at least two or three madmen should be included amongst the company, those who will mutilate their food as they eat it, and spit on the table as their eyes roll around in their heads as others nibble on their thumbs with uncertain anxiety.

There is nothing more revolting than to see wine drunk out of goblets or glasses.

Brisk wines should be served in *tazzini*, and drunk with a counter-point of gravity, in the manner of Abyssinian priests.

Honey can ritualistically be rubbed over the cup before drinking.

To demonstrate vocation, white wine can be
flavored with cowslips.

When offering someone a dish, pronounce its
name with a lisp.

If one cannot garnish a dish with pearls or
emeralds, one should not garnish it at all.

One should always keep a remedy for
excitement near the dinner table.

Never whisper.

Never wash dishes with soap, as then
everything will taste like soap.

Place a container of rhubarb powder on the
table in the place of pepper. Pepper is revolting
and should never be eaten, even by the most
transgressive.

Rise up early every morning and wash the eyes
in rose water.

The only thing black pepper is good for is killing flies.

Many people like vomit, so never expect to be appreciated.

The German method for preventing excitement is the most efficacious.

COOKING AUSTRALIA

Colby Smith

Australia is a paradox: both country and continent, prison and haven, populous and uninhabitable. It is both a superpower and a footnote. A miracle and a disgrace.

Since the dawn of recorded dreaming, the population of the paradox have consumed and been consumed. They were both chef and entrée before the megafauna vanished. *Megalania prisca*, named by Sir Richard Owen in 1859, was the apex predator of the paradox. A monitor lizard the length of a municipal bus—an anachronism from Hell—it probably dined on humans. However, like most of the novel fauna native to the paradox, the humans revolted against their predator, and the monster went extinct some 50,000 years ago. It is unknown whether *Megalania* was hunted or if its extinction was the byproduct of friendly competition, but for the sake of argument it must be granted that it was hunted. Paleoanthropologists know that the humans living on the paradox used fire. The beast was cooked.

The prey dreams, and continues to dream even after it is digested and shat out. Human waste contains grains of memories from the realm of dreams. The flies that consume the dream-laced dung become intoxicated with the images of everything its originator has eaten; for the short life of flies, the experience is more potent than the strongest hallucinogen, more fulfilling than the deepest ritual.

Captain Cook, as his name implies, was even more voracious: devouring the thylacine and her cubs, bringing dogs and cats to the banquet, swallowing the land itself and all who lived on it.

Conscious consumption here has a ceiling: the targeted obsolescence of a graft culture. Someone with their enteric mind "dreamed" that there were crocodiles, wombats, funnel web spiders, scenic rocks and other themes for posters. But the table was erected where gum trees weep and the sun sows melanomas.

Australia woke up one morning and imagined itself, then forgot that it had done so.

Enormous sections of it are still asleep. Shake an old log and twenty Australians will scurry out, having suddenly remembered:

The beaches growing louder.

The zoo-dazed kangaroos and poisoned rabbit caves.

The   sheep-shearing   lanolin-lathered larrikins.

Culture peeling off land like a cheap bandage on an infected wound.

The Australians were quick to roast any angry penguins they found. This was not because they prized the taste, but because they hungered instead for its absence: demanded pap, nostalgia and songs on the banjo.

There   are   eighteen   human   beings in Australia; the rest are paid actors with investments in gold.

An Australian dessert was once declared for a dancer. It was whipped and frothy, like a dying man's spittle. For the frosting, some tall poppies were milked. Sometimes it still appears in public.

And now some shuffling of the table is necessary.

Lance Adelaide.

Shake Melbourne until it settles.

Dispose of Perth with as much uranium as possible.

Sydney must be wheeled out on a tray beforehand, desperate as it is for inspection: all airs and towers. Weeping Victorian facades, like a pompous tiered cake.

Pull down your hat, be careful of the flies. And toss some chips to the gulls on your way out.

HEAVENLY VICTUALS

Jessica Sequeira

Perpetual are the Fruits

Melwyn bit into an apricot. Perched on his
bejewelled divan, languorous in his golden
tunic, every day he was served the choicest of
delicacies; yet he had begun to feel a certain
boredom. The pumpkin pudding, semolina
dough in clotted cream, and sweet buns were
alright, and the fresh fruits were nothing to
shake a stick at, especially those ripe honeyed
figs.

But what he was craving, truly craving, was
salt. He dreamt of a great mound of it, coarse
grains against finer ones, as on his knees he
pressed his tongue against the briny tip, deeper
and more satisfying than the navel of a dancer.

Nobody else around him seemed to suffer
as he did; his wife was delicately plucking an

orange section from a silver platter, as his two
daughters bit into a watermelon. He supposed
that his mother-in-law was about somewhere,
making headway with a pineapple.

He closed his eyes and tried to concentrate
on the goodness of where he was, since heaven
is all about the positive emotions, but the only
thing he could think about was this mound.

As if summoned, a small jinn appeared.
"Shall I bring you up something spicy with
cumin and fenugreek, or would you prefer your
salt in the shape of a yoghurt drink?" it inquired
with consummate professionalism.

Melwyn sat up, startled. Since where he'd
been sent every wish is immediately fulfilled, he
found himself bringing a spoonful of curried
lentil soup to his burning lips. Besidef him the
rivers increased their trickle to a torrent, and
above him a ficus tree gave a shiver; the taste
was exquisite.

Seeing his pleasure, the jinn did a short
dance of delight, patted its stomach, and
vanished.

Over the coming days (or were they weeks?
seconds? minutes?—time prances and capers)
Melwyn longed again and again for salt, and
each time he was immediately served by this

obliging creature. He tried all sorts of novel delicacies but always the longing remained, which could not be sated.

At last the jinn visited again to soothe his cravings, and by and by the visits became regular.

Melwyn suspected that something in this arrangement, in which the creature seemed to receive hidden messages almost before he himself knew what he wanted, and to arrive by the most ingenious methods of transport, was mildly dubious in its righteousness.

Yet the Lofty One must have been aware, even if he turned a blind eye, omnipotent as he was. Perhaps for him too, perfection meant desire, followed by meals of salt, without such sugary conclusiveness. After all, did not salt make one thirsty; was not salt desire itself?

At first, Melwyn proceeded cautiously, but as the menus grew more complex, promising further and greater delights—the turning point was a plate of lemony moutabal into which he dipped soft pita triangles, accompanied by plump black olives—Melwyn could take no more.

Confident in his words, he spoke to the jinn the next time he saw him: "Release me from this syrupy hell," he requested.

The jinn looked at him with a twinkle in his eye and nodded.

In a flash Melwyn was in hellfire, amidst flames tinged carmine by lithium chloride, once used as a replacement for table salt though today considered lightly toxic.

The Lofty One thundered out: "Look, I am an understanding chap, but to remain here your good deeds must outweigh your sins. You have craved salt more than you have sweet, and for this you shall suffer."

Melwyn listened, and for a moment an image came to him of his daughter, her hand trembling as she held out to him a bowl of rosewater ice cream.

Yet quickly it passed, as for the first time he tucked into his first course, tasting the subtle wonders of fruits from the other side: smoked peaches with salt, avocados with salt, grapefruits with salt, tomatoes with salt, cantaloupes with salt . . .

THE VERTICAL TABLE

Justin Isis

We are used to encountering the table as a necrophile encounters a corpse: vulnerable in repose, courting decay. Everything is supine, limply accessible, liable to rot. This persistently two-dimensional arrangement has led us, like the sloppy enthusiast of the deceased, to embrace the most ghastly passivity. Dead matter arranges itself for our convenience in a horizontal tableau, without the bracing tonic of an active gravity. Resistance is necessary for tension and development, yet the modern table presents us with none: sluggish digestion results, and we leave as unsatisfied as we arrived.

Strictly considered, the horizontal table still indecently displayed in our homes is a relic of the 20th century, ill-suited to our current existence and spiritually reeking of a hospital ward in which any dribbling convalescent is welcome to bother us. Approaching the table, we start by lowering ourselves, submitting to chairs, which lock us in place (properly speaking, one defecates while seated or squatting, but one does not eat in this position, much less concern oneself with the psychic effluents of other consumers). Tedious mouths appear in space, and we pick and prod at bits of meat and pieces of plants—conveniently sectioned and segregated, drizzled with dressings—while fielding all manner of fatuous impositions and maudlin reminiscences, the fortification of our flesh constantly interrupted by secondhand opinions, unsupportable politics and intolerable solicitations. Our spirits become flattened and distended as we chew, and our minds film over with a scum of sentiment. The whole thing usually ends with a resigned indulgence in cheap wine, cocaine of dubious purity, desserts that are little more than defrosted clots of refined sugar, and whatever other palliatives are on hand. Televisions glower behind us, waiting like lampreys to attach their monitor-mouths to our postprandial weakness.

It is too much to hope for an expansive apartment or secluded estate. It is too much even to expect solitude. Most of us come to hunger surrounded by our lovers, our children, whatever conspirators and collaborators we deem necessary. But we must not let them interrupt our delectation, and we must not interrupt theirs. Rather, arrangements must be made to discourage talk and encourage focused consumption. The table must be reformulated: the supine corpse must spring to life and stand.

The vertical table need not be a luxury item. A simple sheet of metal will do: rectangular, firmly-supported, rising from floor to ceiling. The arrangement of dishes will resemble something an artful shrike might construct: delicacies fixed in place, impaled on spikes and pins. Various braziers may be inserted or suspended in place, heating the items directly above them, warming those around them with an ambient glow. More elaborate tables with sliding sections will become glorious culinary cabinets resembling a lady's bureau, packed with compartments full of exotic condiments and unexpected side dishes. Circumambulation of the table will reveal new angles from which to consider the relationships between items, new perspectives on their improvised yet integrated system.

The vertical table: the meal as Ascension, as focused conquest. Each item, pinned in place, will draw attention to those above it, encouraging a simple, timely progression and eliminating the need for multiple courses with oppressive cutlery and superfluous dishes. One might start with earthy staples—potatoes, perhaps—easily accessible at waist level, before moving on to the animal flesh and vegetables situated above them, at last arriving at airier, sweeter delights in the higher regions. The abolition of plates will allow for immediate correspondences between items, sudden and shifting constellations of flavor. The juice from a ripe mandarin may drip onto a bit of lightly-seared steak, while chillies, artfully sliced, scatter seeds of fire on the sliced apples below, and cubes of skewered pork slide into votive bowls of raw yolk: vitalizing emanations; novel configurations of sour and savoury, hot and cold. The system of the meal will stand revealed with all its subtle interconnections.

It is best to dine on utterly fresh meats and vegetables and to serve them mostly raw. We suggest:

A bull's heart on a spike, drizzled with lemon juice.

Oysters, gently agitated so that they threaten to slip from their shells.

Thinly-sliced salmon and tuna, acquainted with white pepper.

A ball of mozzarella, pinioned, obese.

Figs and dates, dusted with cocoa.

A fan of livers.

Candied pineapple.

Rose petals.

Fried information.

Curtains of tripe.

Roasted crickets.

Diverse fermented notions.

Salted lobster tails.

Wasp honey.

Wine-soaked watermelon.

Vintage prayers.

A cleansing sorrow, the consistency of shaved ice.

Desserts should be placed in the uppermost reaches of the table, barely within reach: cinnamon sticks; small speared tarts; saucers of cream with floating raspberries, liable to spill on the heads of the unwary and unfocused who lack the dexterity to reach them. Mashed pears. Pomegranate ice cream.

The attitude of approach is essential; one should be hungry enough to pluck the eyes from a deer in mid-leap. It should be necessary not only to stand, but to strain one's arms upward, seizing delicacies as if from the branches of a steel tree, forcing the aspirational posture of a mendicant reaching for sustenance: eating while standing, while moving, while dancing. Conversation should mostly be discouraged, or limited to discussion of which items to taste next. Screens of all kinds should be banished: there is nothing more revolting than a roomful of stuffed spectators gnawing on bland nonsense while numbed by the latest serial drama or streaming inanity.

The horizontal table: lethargy; the Fall; assumption of the Death Posture while feeding. The vertical table: lightness, liberation and athleticism: a return to active physical engagement.

The vertical table: prime rampart of the Neo-Decadent fortress of consumption: also improvised gallery wall, anatomical exhibition of vitalizing forces.

We will resurrect the corpse of the table as a shining monument to our own appetites. Passéists still dining horizontally will be mocked and shunned as ghoulish throwbacks.

Standing erect, we will embrace the luxurious rapacity of our existence, so that we may grow strong and breed as all ravenous things must: locusts; missionaries; dissenting opinions; sunflowers with bright brown faces and crowns of insolent gold, their spirits those of drunken jesters mocking the ugly solemn sky.

LONDON IN THREE COURSES: SECOND COURSE

David Rix

Pass west under the bridge from St Pancras Basin, the bridge where the long bullet trains from the continent boom like the largest bass drum in history, and you will find a hidden garden. Not hidden from view, though most ignore it, but hidden from access. It lies at the foot of high walls of dingy London brick and is entirely hemmed in by water—the only way to reach here being to tie up by boat.

And here it was that I found the Wandering Eye.

I double-moored her and stepped ashore, noting various changes that had taken place in the garden since I was last here. Lauren had been at work, it seemed. It had her signature. A few new figures—sculptures—new paintings on the brickwork. Not that this was her place, by any means. Such a place could not, or should not belong to anyone. But sometimes, if you are lucky, you have places that feel like home—that you can stamp yourself onto. And this was one of hers.

There was also an elephant, I realised. Stone. Familiar. Old and worn—not a recent work. Possibly it was the one I had saved from East Cross, but I wasn't sure.

I turned at the sound of gentle swirling water, as Lauren came drifting up in a canoe, loaded down with shopping and nets. Since I had double-moored her, she grabbed my gunwale and slung the bags onto my deck while I hurried to help. When boats tie up side by side, there is no choice but for one to become the porch of the other.

"We tying alongside for a bit again?" she asked.

"May I?"

"Of bloody course," she said, settling with a sigh of relief in one of the chairs in the little garden. "Give me a drink, Liqueur Man, and I'll cook dinner. Later."

I scrambled back inside the Eibonvale and returned with a bottle.

"Oh, wow," Lauren said. And this was indeed a rather special bottle. A dizzying drink brewed over a period of years with no less than thirty-seven of the Hackney ingredients—a soft green fluid with a scent that could make colours dance in your eyes. An underworld or waterworld chartreuse that personally I preferred, though few knew of its existence. This was a drink that didn't even have a number.

"To long moorings and quiet waters," I said and the glasses met with a clink.

"To tying up alongside—forever and always," she countered with a knowing grin.

We sipped in silence—such a drink demanded silence—and for a while the tranquillity was absolute. Even the bullet trains, even the passers-by on the towpath across the water couldn't penetrate it. It was a perfect moment when sound was just not needed.

"Hello?"

Another gentle splashing from the canal and I leaned to see round the two boats. It was one of the floating tents being gently piloted towards us with a roughly carved oar. He raised his hand in greeting.

"Mind if I tie up here for a bit?" the occupant asked.

"Of course not," Lauren said with a smile.
"They keep steeling my blankets."

"Who do?" I asked.

"I wish I knew. Some land-bound yobs."

Lauren swore sympathetically and helped him sling a rope round one of the moorings. He was a tall and rather skinny man, somewhat oversized for the small tent. His clothes old and well-sewn, his hair with that unkempt wildness that comes from living removed from any normal facilities.

"Spare any food?" he asked. "I can trade something I think you'll like. You know—always good to have a varied diet."

"Maybe," Lauren said. "I have some crayfish about ready. And a big fat carp. And a bladderwort salad."

"Bladderwort?" I asked with interest, and she nodded. Bladderwort—the carnivorous waterplant that catches small creatures using hollow chambers that open at a touch and suck in its prey. I had eaten it a few times, having been alerted to it as a foodstuff by a rather entertaining argument over whether it was suitable for vegans, and liked it a lot. It was number 108 on my list of liqueurs. Not seen very often around London, however.

He chuckled, reached into the open tent and pulled out a bucket. "Take a look at this."

I leaned over. It was full of long, thin black wriggling . . .

"Wow," I said, exchanging glances with Lauren. "Horse leeches."

Each about ten or twelve centimetres long.

Lauren laughed quietly. "Okay . . . I'd have shared anyway but now you can *definitely* join us."

"If you can allow me access to a pan, may I cook them for you?" he asked with a surprisingly regal politeness.

"By all means," Lauren said. "And I will prepare the carp. We shall have a feast. And we can tell our stories."

Chopped leech, or even whole leeches quickly seared, is quite a delicacy and again quite rare around the city. They can make a nice chewy morsel, or can be ground up with spices to make nuggets—very appetising when breaded and fried brown. Most prefer to cook them slim, keeping them as long as necessary to achieve that end. Some, however, like to cook them fat, very nutritious, and the resulting dish has a predictable hint of black pudding about it. The bloody leeches are simply known as leech loaf when minced and formed into the right shape.

The only thing to remember is never ever to eat them alive. They can sucker on and continue their lives quite well inside you.

I helped him out of the floating tent and into the tiny garden.

"Elephant," he murmured, coming to a stop and staring at the sculpture with a strangely fascinated expression.

"Yes," Lauren said. "We saved this one from demolition in Hackney Wick."

He nodded. "Every so often, an elephant. They give me hope."

I watched him curiously.

"How so?" Lauren asked.

"Maybe it's a symbol of something," he said. "The elephants have a long memory—maybe that's comforting for forgotten people. At the very least, it is a symbol of all the many, many levels that exist in this city, with the cruelty of the normal nothing more than a surface froth. It just makes me think that somewhere, someone . . . remembers."

There was a silence—a melancholy silence. In the middle-distance, one of the sleek bullet trains crossed the bridge, heading for the continent. They travelled fast and far, those trains, yet I remained singularly un-envious. A world that progresses at about four miles per hour, a world where there is time to think and to remember, is no bad thing, I believe.

SOME NECESSARY WORDS ON THE SUBJECT OF FRUIT

Quentin S. Crisp

I have been asked to talk about fruit, and I won't pretend I don't know why. It is because of my longstanding aversion, of which you have perhaps heard. The aversion has been exaggerated, naturally, but it is quite real. I say "aversion" rather than "phobia"—my feelings towards fruit are not those, for instance, of an arachnophobe towards spiders. Nor is it the case that I would simply prefer to avoid the consumption of fruit as a matter of taste. I will not stop here to reflect on how much the word "phobia" has been abused, no; let me simply confess—or proclaim—my feelings: I do not want to be in the vicinity of certain species of fruit. The smell, the sight, the presence, the thought of them, all fill me with revulsion and abhorrence.

Again, let me be quite candid—I am only human and there are some species of fruit that I will eat. However, I would rather not name these. It is a curious thing, but if I name to others any variety of fruit I consider safe, it is likely thereafter to make the uncanny transition into the other zone—of the nameable but untouchable.

Since I can name the worst of the fruit kingdom, then—name those that are unlikely ever to be redeemed—I will do so. They are oranges, apples, bananas and grapes. Apart from these, there are others that remain ambiguous, in a kind of fructiferous purgatory, though it is possible they too will eventually be consigned to that singularity of loathsomeness from which escape is almost or entirely impossible.

You will ask me to explain myself. It is at this point that I must cease to speak in a direct and systematic manner. My feelings towards, my understanding of, the fruits that I have named, belong to what is called "the primitive". They cannot be described in terms of anything else. Yet it is true those feelings and that understanding are related to many things, and I must hint through these relations, by recounting certain facts and circumstances drawn from life that are nonetheless indistinguishable from fable, and by making cryptic gestures of image.

What are apples, then, if not the entrails of womankind? By some mockery, they have been made crisp so that they preserve the tooth-marks of those who bite. Take a pocket knife and halve an apple—you see a sectioned womb. The hollow at the centre contains seed. Exposed to air, these innards oxidise, reminding us how quickly fertility spoils. The very sweetness of the fruit is incipient corruption. It summons insects. Their banquet is decay.

Was the apple the first innuendo? Some seem to think so, and if we cast our eye liberally over the world of rumour that is art, we find the seduction of Eden echoed with other fruits and in other ways in books, paintings, songs and, now, films. In such territory, I feel cold and alien. These fruit-themed jokes do little to stimulate my funny bone, and nothing is more likely to render me a devout Christian than the threat of seduction with fruit. A cold shower in holy water is called for, not to cool me off, but to wash away the thought of stickiness.

I am envious, they will say; no, repulsed, I will reply. It does not matter—let us grant both. The fact is, in either case, I cannot understand those who find the fruit seductive, those who give themselves up to it. It is shamelessness and, for better or worse, I am not shameless. Worse? Well, I need not explain that. The world at present flees from shame. But better? Yes, I think I might be better in some way for knowing shame. After all, what is the shamelessness that I am said to envy but a vacuity? There is no way for me to enter into such a thing. It seems for me as if it has no inside. It is the case for me simply that to exist is to be in exile from vacuity, from shamelessness, and this exile is revulsion and shame and, yes, you may believe it and titter, envy.

I am forced now to speak of oranges. What an incomparable fruit! I have heard the tasting of an orange cited, many times, as an experience beyond description, and a token of the value of experience itself. Yet, who are these that consume an orange in the presence of others? If I enter a train carriage and sit, and someone at the far end of the carriage, behind me, digs a thumbnail into the skin of an orange, I know upon the instant, and will exit. The smell penetrates and permeates, worse than that of dead fish. Those who have eaten the fruit have shimmering scales on their fingers. Once or twice in my life someone has embraced me in this condition and I have shuddered, then and for some time after.

Yet oranges are not the worst. The worst, by far, is the banana. A strange shadow is cast upon my existence, as you know, by Quentin Crisp, the author of *The Naked Civil Servant*. Early in that book he chooses to describe his father as the kind of person who would eat a banana with a knife and fork. To contemporary eyes, says that other Crisp, this is "a dead giveaway". I am not interested, however, in what this habit says about Crisp's father, but what it says about bananas. We feel discomfort at the thought of a banana being eaten with knife and fork like other food. Some would dispense with the knife and fork. This is the wrong move. We would do better to dispense with the banana. The discomfort is not an indication that we should cast aside all decorum. No, it means that somewhere in the chaos of our inner being a sensitive and knowing instrument responds with detestation even to contact through a piece of cutlery with the obscenely yielding pulp of that most degrading of all berries—of all edible objects.

Many humans have come to disregard the warnings of that inner instrument. I, however, cannot.

On grapes, I would prefer not to comment at all. Let me only say this: please do not bring them if you are visiting me in hospital. This strange, old custom still lingers, I think. But grapes are not the kind of token that will encourage me to health.

In general, though, grapes are permissible when they have been thoroughly crushed and transformed into wine, or dried into raisins. Similarly, apples are permissible if thoroughly baked in a pie or crumble until all crispness has gone. Cider, however, like apple juice, is to be avoided.

I can never make my stipulations thoroughly enough, and in sufficient detail, that people will understand. Knowing this in advance, I will limit myself to the above suggestions.

I want to return to that remark of Crisp, that his father's habit was "a dead giveaway". Having written this much, I can't escape the suspicion that readers will take all this to be the rankest

Freudianism. This notion exasperates me. Does it not occur to people that if something can symbolise sex, then sex can, in turn, symbolise something else?

What most concerns me, when I see someone, with utter complacency, peel a banana in a lecture hall or on the Tube, is the lack of shame. I don't understand this need, since some time last century, to be proud of every appetite one has. Public spaces are not made more beautiful by exhibitionism. Must we hear everyone's confessions? Are these even confessions—are they not boasts? And we are expected not only to hear, but to applaud, as if these boasting-confessions are salvation itself.

The person without shame is a person without sensitivity. This statement is so easily misunderstood, I have long hesitated to make it. Because implicit in this, though too often forgotten, is the fact that to use a person's shame against him or her is a vulgar cruelty—it is, itself, a shameless act. In mutual shame is kindness.

I know, I know. That kind of kindness is too roundabout and troublesome—having to second-guess each other all the time (whatever "second-guess" means). The future of humankind is in unilaterally peeling bananas on trains. Quite so. Quite so. But it is a future without literature. And—I am resigned to it—without me.

THE IMMACULATE SCRAMBLED AUTOMAT

Damian Murphy

1

Nadja dreamed of iron madams in sleek, magnetic brothels, aristocratic automatons controlled by atmospheric impulses, conspiracies of teletype and magnetic recording tape, and a runaway electric tram sent hurtling through the strata of the earth. She rose from a bed in an old hotel, retrieved a perfectly preserved egg from the icebox, set it on the surface of a saucer of titanium, and crept down a hallway to its terminal end. She placed the dish on the floor beneath a spyhole set low into the wall. It was impossible to look through without kneeling. The glass was stained with a patina of milky film, on the other side of which could just be made out an older woman talking on the telephone. Her voice was swallowed up in silence.

Later, upon returning, she found that the egg had not been altered in the least. Pulling the saucer away from the wall, she peered through the glass once more. The view revealed nothing but an empty apartment. She'd spent hours searching for an entrance to the space on the other side. The room seemed to be impregnable, or at least impossible to access from the inside of the building. She returned to the room she'd claimed as her own, determined to try again the following evening. The process would continue until the cycle was complete.

2

My Dearest Ludwig, Imperial Vizier of the Imperium Hotel,

Sometimes she's older and sometimes she's younger. On other occasions, it seems she's hardly there at all. Once I spied her pressed up flat against the wall, her body almost entirely camouflaged by the pattern on the wallpaper. I suspect she spies on me as well.

Her telephone is doubtless unconnected to the grid. I've seen her writing manifestoes on the floor before the bed in a language comprised of inkblots connected with barely-visible threads. She is a priestess, a poet, a prostitute, and a trespasser. I don't believe that she belongs in the apartment at all.

Her influence, if my theories prove correct, is purely literary. It perpetuates itself by obfuscation and duplicity. I feel that I've almost captured it. A little time is all I need. I still have several methods at my disposal. I'll keep you posted, but not by way of another letter. I'm certain that she intercepts them.

Once I've succeeded in preparing my egg, I'll present it to the Automat. Then we shall see.

In whatever shreds of dignity are left to us and in our ability to fake it when need be,

Your beloved Nadja

3

The Automat's voice was hopelessly distorted from a general lack of maintenance. One would not be advised to sample the delicacies in its discoloured glass compartments. It had long been plagued with an infestation of moths, yet this didn't hamper its operation in any noticeable way. Nadja had written down a series of commands issued forth from the amplifier above the pie racks:

"TRANS-MIT-MAG-NET-IC-DREEM-CY-FER"

"PROH-PITCH-EE-ATE-THEE-NITE-WACH"

"CUN-SOOM-UN-END-ING-SIG-NEL-TRANS-FUR"

"UN-LEESH-ETH-EER-IC-NITE-DRUM-SEE-KWENSE"

She'd tallied its instructions, arranged the syllables in columns and applied deductive algebra, permuted them according to the protocols of ancient oracles, and determined what it was she thought it wanted. Curiosity compelled her, yet there was something else as well. She wanted to taste of the unspeakable pleasures unveiled in her dreams.

4

She shoved her latest letter through the grille before one of the heating vents. She often sat and listened at the openings. The distant rise and fall of voices echoed through the metal chambers. Somewhere, perhaps in the upper reaches near the penthouse, could be heard the resonant grind and rattle of the shifting of gears.

She returned to her egg at the end of the hallway and peered through the spyhole once more. The initial blackness cleared like a mist, giving way to several images superimposed on one another: black latex gloves pulled up to the elbow caressed a typewriter with missing keys; a lamp that shone without a bulb emitted streams of deadly vapor; cassette reels clicked and a monocle shattered, showering a leather mask with tiny shards of glass. Somehow the images refused to coalesce into a comprehensive narrative. They surged and flickered, shifting rapidly to either side, occasionally warping like a strip of overheated celluloid. She couldn't bring herself to watch for more than a minute or two. The pallid light in which the images were suffused produced a tiny spot of pain behind her brow.

She suspected that the sequence was nearly complete. Her egg was radiant with a potent and diabolical ethero-magnetic vibration. She could sense its influence, invisible and odorless, in the extremities of the hotel. It even affected the surrounding wallpaper, giving rise to a rich discolouration that brought out its nascent excess. Within a couple of days it would be fully cooked.

5

Rev. Bartholomew Francis, Grand Diplomat and Spy of the Imperium Hotel,

I can say with reasonable certainty that our rooms are connected, hers and mine. At first, I thought it was only a matter of finding a secret entrance, but as it turns out it's far more involved than that. The space itself is shared, though the context is kept separate by relative degrees of rotation. I've managed on occasion to bring them nearly into alignment by way of strategic rearrangements, arduous rites, and eroto-comatose lucidity.

I have every reason to believe that she passes back and forth from one apartment to the other while I'm sleeping. She's quite adept at making the transition, while I have yet to effect it even once myself. Were I to succeed in doing so, I'm not so sure that I could find my way back. So far as I can tell, her room isn't equipped with so much as a single exit.

In response to the question that you hadn't thought to ask, the operation is proceeding nicely. I've been slowly preparing the Automat, lulling it into a soft magnetic relay state in order to make it more receptive to fluctuations in the astral light. My technique is simple, yet potent. It involves calligraphy and mirrors. The results are painted onto pages torn from technical manuals, then rolled up and placed into the empty compartments in the Automat's exterior.

I cannot possibly hope to fill all of them. There are thousands on the entry floor alone and thousands more that can't be reached. The Automat is clearly at least seven stories high and who knows how far it extends beneath the surface of the earth. There are countless dangers attendant to the higher floors. Even the ground floor requires careful navigation.

I once began to fashion a map, but that incorrigible woman came to steal it while I was out. I've seen it since in her apartment—she'd left it carelessly lying in full view of the spyhole. I don't think she realises precisely where I watch her from. The lens must be invisible from the inside.

In any case, I impatiently await her next visitation. I've devised a trap that I'm quite certain will ensnare her.

In overwhelming boredom
and exquisite ennui,

Your faithful servant, Nadja

6

Nadja had climbed into the very heart of the Automat. Rusted ladders and crumbling stairs had discouraged further ascent. Flaming lamps in iron frames descended from ropes attached to the ceiling. These were so low to the floor that Nadja had to weave between them as she made her way through the isolated chamber.

In the center of the space was a stainless steel stand that supported an aluminum bowl. A large, rectangular screen had been set into the far wall, the monochrome light that shone from its surface contending with the flicker of the candle flames. The display showed the apartment from an angle that she'd never seen before. The view afforded was higher than that of the spyhole and on the other side of the room.

She appeared there on an exquisitely upholstered armchair. She was resplendent, half-transparent, and as naked as the moon. Cryptographic characters had been inked upon her flesh in an uneven grid of criss-crossing lines. She must have circumvented every one of the traps that had been carefully laid out for her. She appeared to be gazing directly at Nadja through the slight warp of the screen.

With a hand at once reverent, nervous, and defiant, Nadja placed her egg in the bowl. She could sense the dark, magnetic pulse as it passed through the silverware that lay to either side. The woman smoked her cigarette from her place upon the armchair, her face a mask of sensual excitement. Nadja was certain that she'd find her mistress waiting for her when she returned to her own room. She simply stood amidst the lamps as the light begin to fade, the image on the screen slipping back into the blackness of a sleeper on the edge of oblivion.

REVOLT OF
THE KITCHENS

Jessica Sequeira

You've asked for my report as head chef on the events that shook Above and Below, and fundamentally cast doubt on the nature of food delivery, among other questions. What happened still disturbs me, and in a way I'm grateful that you're forcing me to organise my impressions and speak—if only so as never to dwell on such matters again.

Those who don't know better might think everything here is clear-cut, that goodies and baddies go where they deserve, and that's that. Of course, you and I know that things aren't so simple. For starters, along with our bosses who get all the press—the Lofty One and his angel helpers, the Humble One and his nimble djinns—an entire realm of intermediary service workers exists to supply necessaries for both worlds. Food workers belong to this category, as do your sort, police officers.

The kitchens' work is legal and necessary, albeit not publicised. The base of food is the same for everyone, a special shadow mixture that serves as material to be shaped and coloured, an atomic substrate. (The "world" familiar to mortals works in a similar way, but I leave these details to our celestial physicists.)

There have been attempts to mechanise everything, but somehow the artisanal approach still produces superior results. So we work away, us experts, the chefs of the here-not-here, kneading and rolling and whipping and frying and stirring and giving the whole caboodle a good flip.

As you know, of course, there's a lot that both Higher-Ups and Lower-Downs would prefer to keep covered up. A healthy contraband trade exists between realms for whatever one's taste might be, from spicy to sweet-salty. People aren't supposed to get hold of certain foods, but somehow they do. I just try to make sure it doesn't come out of the kitchens I manage. Such shenanigans have never seen me involved, but I've been in the business long enough to recognize the stink of rot at the slightest whiff.

A fair amount of chef swiping goes on too. Everyone wants the very best. In mortal life I was head honcho at a posh restaurant in Chile, where *santiaguinos* who fancied themselves Parisians (the kind who don't exist in Paris) skewered olives and cheese with toothpicks, stabbed forks into expensively perched salads, and savoured our delicate homemade raviolis, irrigating their bellies with long-stemmed glasses of wine, poured down the hatch. Not to mention the chocolate crème brûlée, exquisite. At that place I employed only the most-qualified and best-trained, the ones who were technically capable but also imaginative, not just chefs but also poets. Of course, my competitors wanted the same, and would resort to underhanded tactics to pinch my culinary artists. It wasn't just money they offered, but write-ups in magazines, better quality ingredients, airtime on popular daytime cooking shows.

When I got here, in my capacity as inter-realm service worker—which didn't surprise me, as I'd never thought of myself as quite admirable or vile enough for either Higher-Up or Lower-Down—I assumed things would be different. My greatest surprise was how similar everything is to our earthly world, except perhaps for a slight increase in appetites; celestial beings require hefty portions. But there's all the same trafficking, and the same chef snatching—you can turn a blind eye, as the omnipotent ones surely do, but a tipping point was inevitable.

The revolt had probably been brewing for some time before it reached us. As I've already said, I'm quick to notice when something is going on under my nose, beyond the usual simmering of stew and baking of bread. My first suspicion, as usual, was either contraband or chef snatching, and quickly my suspicions began to favour the latter.

A new chef, Emilia, had appeared in our midst. She was beautiful, with dark hair and blue eyes, and a strip of blue silk wrapped around her head. No relationships are permitted here; if anything happens, the parties are sent together to some other place. We're expected to turn all our passions towards food, the shadow food we make and mould and colour and send out with the messengers.

This chef, however, behaved oddly. First off, she flirted with us old-timers in a way we thought antiquated, belonging to the mortal world. What was she trying to achieve? It soon became clear, or so I thought, when I caught her slipping away with my best chef Alonso, at a moment that she assumed I was giving sautée tips to new recruits. She led him to a corridor by the storage rooms in the huge labyrinth where we work. Pressing against him, the smooth blue silk of her headdress touched his rough skin, and I could see he was fascinated. She whispered something in his ear that made his eyes open wide, like the dinner plates we send to the fanciest folks in both regions.

"Hold it right there," I said. At that moment I felt a bit like you, a cop. It was unpleasant, to be honest. "Stop the charade. I know you're trying to swipe my chef."

Startled, Alonso pushed her off and leapt up. "It isn't what it looks like, sir," he said. "Emilia was just telling me . . ." and he blushed.

"What was she telling you?" I asked coldly. When it's needed, I can flash a look that will freeze a custard.

Emilia reacted. She tried to cover his mouth with her hand, but he pushed it away. "She said the tunnels of these kitchens lead not only to other kitchens, where she worked before, but also to a tunnel that can get us out. She found out about it, it's why she was expelled from her last job. There's a way to take me back to my wife and two daughters, at least a way I can try. It's not that I'm unhappy here, sir, but please understand . . ."

This was not going to end well, Emilia realised immediately. Before I could stop her, she'd unfurled the blue silk from her head and flung it into the air. In the moment we were blinded by its wave of blue, she darted down the hallway and disappeared without a trace.

Alonso and I looked at the blue silk on the ground. I was afraid to pick it up, even to touch it. I had no idea where Emilia had come from, or if what she'd said was true; she'd simply appeared in our kitchen one day. We'd always been told we would work in the kitchens to the end of time, at best transferred from one to another—that there was no exit. For the first time, like Alonso, I started to have my doubts.

I tried to convince myself the incident was a one-time act of madness by a disillusioned staff member. But she wasn't the only one. Word got round there were other women in blue silk headdresses performing acts of metaphysical seduction. Discontent rumbled in the kitchens, and the other head chefs and I knew something was going to explode.

The day of events, I'd come in early to make sure everything was spick-and-span. Conventional time doesn't exist here, but I suppose celestial beings have retained it for our convenience, since it's certainly easier to boil an egg or keep pasta *al dente* if you can count in human minutes. The first thing I noticed was that every surface, from faucets to counters, had been wrapped in strips of blue silk. The place was so blue it was impossible to see even a hint of steel underneath; intruders must have got in.

I'd been afraid of touching the blue silk before, but now I was angry. With my bare hand, I went to peel the fabric away from the table. It came off easily, and I thought of flinging it down the garbage chute that debouches into lower realms. But the cloth stayed close to my hand, slithering around it in sinuous shapes. It seemed to rustle and beckon me forwards, out the kitchen and down corridors I'd never visited before.

I was scared, but also fascinated; I had no idea where I was going, but had ceased to care. Inspector, I assure you this fascination was a very peculiar one, which I've never felt before or since.

Following that blue silk, I found myself in a giant open space where I recognised several other chefs, including Alonso. All of us had blue silk twining round our wrists and bodies. The rustle of it was so enticing, you can't even imagine.

The arena began to fill with more and more of us. It swelled with emotion, with a sense of impending freedom, with desire to head home to our loved ones, or at least back to another place than the usual kitchens. We began to sing louder and louder, in a kind of chant with just one lyric: *Take us there. Eternity is hell.*

This, I suppose, is when the guards were alerted. By following the blue silk, they found the mass of us with blue silk on our arms. I'd caught a glimpse of Emilia and some other women in the crowd, but now they disappeared.

Were they infernal agents, bearers of contraband truth, or chef swipers whose seductive lies had a far greater effect than anticipated? I still don't know; I don't know what to believe at all anymore. It's probable I'll keep cooking these shadow meals in the kitchens forever. Only now have I realised the inter-realm does not exist, and that we're in hell or at least purgatory.

Sir, you too work in the inter-realm. Don't you think this alone justifies what you call a revolt? Take this bit of gorgeous blue silk and tell me honestly.

THE WILD HUNT

Douglas Thompson

What is the recipe for woman and for man? I am
not a chef but a psychopomp, from the ancient
Greek, a guider of the souls of the dead towards
the afterlife. Or am I Wotan, Odin, Herod
or Auld Nick, or some higher authority from
another world, who craves the taste of terrestrial
flesh? There is a storm brewing, a swirling of
clouds, and so I and my host of demons and
demigods and demagogues fill the sky with
our rising howling as we circumnavigate the
stratosphere, in search of what?

For the seed, the fruit, the quintessence of
course, of dust. Of cock and hen, cock and bull,
cock and cunt. Cock our guns, we big game
hunters, as we billow along the burgeoning
gun-metal grey clouds, pregnant with imminent
rainfall, drooping like wrinkled old dugs ower

yer heids. Ten score whores are we, witches, bitches. We crave the taste of mortal life, the ephemera, rain down our reign on all ye down below.

Lenticular stratus, cumulonimbus, the monstrous grey drips of our cloak-clouds reach down, some spin into twisters to drop and rip up the land and transport a few unlucky fortunates skyward. We are black crows, magpies of Man, on the look-out, to scavenge for the residue of consciousness, the leavened bread of the wheat and chaff of this earth, the human poppies who grow tall and sway their bulb-like heads in the sun, hollow eyes turned upwards awaiting us, meaning resolution, attainment, release; meaning death. Life is confinement. We, the alien host, are come to set you free.

What is the recipe of woman and of man? Here it is. A pinch of dirt, of mandrake, the semen of hanged men, the crushed shells of some beetles, a dozen lizards' tails. Roses and carnations, dahlias and sarracenias of course, their gloriously treacherous throats bloated with dead wasps. For all in Nature is consumption, foul gluttonous absorption of its own murdered children. Nature is coprophagia. Bring us eyelashes and broomsticks and the hulls of wrecked galleons. Bring us broken church bells and the rusting axles of crashed cars from scrapheaps a mile across. Bring us foxgloves and laburnum, digitalis and quinine. Man is poison. Man is the lethal microbe in the stomach of this earth, who will consume his own host, his own mother, if she doesn't get there first.

Some say it is King Arthur who leads the Wild Hunt, or Gwynn ap Nudd, anti-pope of the netherworld spirit folk, or such infamous dead as Theoderic the Great, or Valdemar Atterdag of Denmark. Deep is human folk memory, darker than Loch Ness or the Mariana Trench, some deep socket where the tooth of Atlantis was long since pulled. Bring us the essence of man, of woman. Bitter black chocolate of the Aztecs and Incas, dried blood of ants of a hundred thousand unjust altardeaths reaching backwards like a red carpet into the grinning skull-teeth of Xibalba and Metnal, Beelzebub and mescal. Swallow that worm that eats its own tail, ouroboros, like the Gods on us, we feed upon ourselves, man and woman, complete the perfect circle, of day and night, of life and death, satiety and hunger. Lick and suck at the cock and the dug.

What is the formula, the genetic code, the DNA spiral, double helix of entwining backbones, of this sculpture of flesh we call the human tree? Plant that grows and picks its own fruit and eats its own shit endlessly. The old die that the young might live. The Wild Hunt is ourselves, the old preying on the young, the young on the old, the strong on the weak, the weak on the strong periodically through the convenient contrivances of politics and sociology. Pedagogy. Pederasty. Cannibalism. Ritualised rape. All of Nature reeks no more or less than we do, of decay and ferment, of death and rebirth.

So your life has been lived in a cycle of contraction? Were the barbarians at the gates? Do our Neros fiddle while our heroes piddle away the warm yellow trickle of their transubstantiated wine? Whine? Must we? The earth pulsates in and out like a terrified sphincter, with all us ants in a panic running circles on it. Rome falls or slides to Constantinople. Jerusalem recants, decants its tents to Blake's London, every slave out of Egypt clanking in mind-forged manacles towards satanic mills, those iron hills, Byronic, bionic, Tennysonic, supersonic, what a tonic, that we are red in tooth and claw with all the rest, the worst, the best of them. We are compost already for all that will come after. Let the Wild Hunt pluck us and taste us from the sky. Let all the panoply of Greek gods fuck us in disguise.

MACHINES THAT EAT FLOWERS

Justin Isis

The man and woman had lived on the island for as long as they could remember. It was their job to care for the garden of metal flowers, to clean the rust from the iron orchids and fill the vases with brittle copper roses. The island was small, but the man and woman were never wanting for anything.

The man's golden hair never wavered in the wind, and the woman's shining silver skin was perfectly cold. No blood beat in their veins, and their unblinking eyes shone only with the sun's reflected glow. When they finished their work for the day, they retreated to the edge of the island and sat on the cliff overlooking the beach, where they watched the waves of acid lapping against the shore. Sometimes they sat in the shade of a gemstone tree, the ground beneath it scattered with sapphires. At night they slept in each other's arms in a field of steel lilies.

Having cohered naturally, they had only a dim sense of the other world, with its green fields, machines of flesh and blood, and other mysteries: a racial memory of the minerals that formed them. The existence they shared was one of constant consumption, that of the island cannibalizing itself, refining base matter. The slow progress of alloys took place inside them, and the production of forms resulted from their daily movements, their shaping of the raw materials on which they walked and slept. By moving and eating and shaping as they did, the matter around them took on its own peculiar life. Sometimes they would mold new flowers with their hands, and at other times they would take the flowers inside them, amalgamating what they needed to grow larger and stronger. They thought of themselves as the island's teeth.

The man had taken to watching the sky, and had noticed that the sun was growing weaker. Usually it pulsed strongest at midday and dimmed at night to a soft luminosity. At noon, at its highest intensity, it cast high-contrast shadows over the brass tulips and scattered a hard bright sparkle across the diamond-studded stalks of the platinum daffodils. But now the light dimmed even during the day. The man and the woman knew the sun's routine by heart, and the recent changes disturbed them.

As the months went by, it became clear that the sun was dying. Sometimes the light would fade entirely, leaving the man and woman stranded in darkness for hours. And the sun's decay spread to the flowers: when the man went to the orchids he found them furred with rust like a fungus, and the copper roses crumbled in his hand. After one long period without light, the orange frost spread even to the flowers in the garden of precious metals. The man and woman knew that gold and platinum were not supposed to rust, but it seemed to them that if the light could fade, anything was possible. Before the failing of the sun, they had known no change.

When darkness fell the man rushed to the woman's side, and they sat and waited for the light to return. At these times they were afraid, but as they drew close to each other they knew they could wait forever. If they stayed together, there was nothing to fear.

At the approach of midsummer the man and woman set out for the beach. They had spent the day gathering the last few untainted roses from the garden of metal flowers, and when they had laid them out on the beach as an offering to the sea, they walked along the shore and scanned the horizon. Just for a moment they felt the sun flicker, as if it had been struck by a sudden convulsion.

They spent the rest of the afternoon gathering flowers from across the island. There were scarcely enough left to form an arrangement. The roses had all but rotted, and most of the orchids crumbled at the touch. Once the man found what he thought to be a perfect silver rose, but when he turned it over he saw a sickly greenish tint spreading across its petals. Its usual fragrance was gone; instead of the sharp scent of silver, there was only a dull metallic odor, the dull greenish stench of mineral decay.

With only a few flowers gathered, they made their way to the cliff overlooking the beach. The cliff face sloped down to a grouping of rocks that soon gave way to sand. The man and woman sat down next to each other and placed the flowers beside them.

The sun stuttered. The wind sang over the sands. For a long time the man could think of nothing to say. Eventually the woman took his hand, and her unchanging eyes rolled towards him. The man lifted her hand and looked at it in the light of the failing sun, examining her nails: chips of jasper. He pressed them to his cheek as he stared out to the sea. The woman's hand moved gently across his face.

They sat for a while in silence, and a resolution grew between them. They did not need to speak it aloud, but both of them knew what they would do.

When dusk fell, the sun began its regular program of reduced intensity. But now its dimness was punctuated by flare-ups of light, sharp stabs like the last beats of a dying heart. The man and woman walked hand-in-hand down to the beach as the light broke around them. In its irregular flashes, they caught sudden frozen views of each other, of the man's golden hair and the woman's silver skin.

They crossed to the shore and saw before them the sterile surface of the waves, transparent like molten glass. The man and the woman turned to each other and at last spoke of what they suspected. Perhaps the island had tired of light, and was retiring the sun for a reason. It was not that the island no longer needed them, they decided: rather, it needed them for something greater than they had ever suspected.

They came within range of the tide. When they felt the acid lapping at their feet, they stopped and turned to each other. Still holding hands, they walked further in and at once understood what was happening: the island was feeding them to the sea, paying homage to its mother by delivering them to the infinite feast at which they would be both consumer and consumed, united forever with all-encompassing existence.

At first they felt only a rising warmth, as if they were stepping into a pool of liquid light. Slowly it spread from their feet up through their legs to the rest of their bodies, caressing their polished flesh. Only when it reached the line of their lips did they feel anything resembling pain, and even then it was only a higher intensity, an ecstasy, like looking at the sun. The sea rushed in through their mouths, their eyes, filling them from the inside, their hands still linked. As the warmth dissolved their other senses they were left with only touch, only the feel of each other's hands.

A strange sensation came over them. They felt as if, rather than the sea entering them, they were passing out of themselves and into it. They tried to focus on the feeling of their linked hands, but it was difficult to remember exactly where they joined, difficult to remember anything. Their awareness faded, lost in the greater warmth.

The man and woman's iron organs corroded slowly. Their polished flesh took longer; for hours afterward, two traceries of silver and gold lingered beneath the waves like sunken statues. Then they dissolved, first breaking into fragments. With their arms eaten away, their clasped hands floated together like a pair of glittering fish. As they drifted down to the sand, the sea picked them apart particle by particle.

The stillness of night settled over the waves. The last light faded, dimmed to black. But the sky did not stay black for long. A brownness like late autumn leaves spread from the dead sun, a colour past death, as if the darkness were rusting. Slowly it filled the sky and crept over the island, until it covered the beach, and the cliff, and the garden of metal flowers.

SEEDS

Ursula Pflug

I don't know how it is I came to have no parents
and no name. I hear this is a place you can
come, if you're looking for a name.

I have nothing. But I have had nothing
before, and now I am glad to be free of it.

It is in the city. There are five of us, or
maybe ten or thirty. The building is an empty
one, gutted by fire. We have been sleeping on
the floors, on found mattresses. I sprayed them
all with a can of bug juice I bought. I do not
like fleas or bedbugs. Since I came here, last
week, I have been planting flowers. I dig the
earth out of the central courtyard. An empty
yard. Probably it is full of lead, but eventually
that too will be washed away by rain. The rain
is cleaner now.

When I came, there was no one here. Now
there are sometimes ten, sometimes twenty of
us. I have planted sunflowers in the yard.

Their big heads turn, slowly, throughout the day.

I make window boxes out of some panelling ripped out of a wall. In them I plant geraniums, herbs and tomatoes. The seeds are seeds I brought from the West. The soil is not good, this soil dug out of the yard. It is not really a yard. One day I wake up and there are chickens in it. Where did the chickens come from? It doesn't matter. They lay eggs, and they will be good to eat, when winter comes.

I gather the chicken dung and dilute it with water, and carefully pour it into the pots of plants. The tomatoes are doing fine. When someone new comes, I make them eat tomatoes.

"Vitamin C," I say. They look at me strange, their eyes wide and dark, blank as stones.

"Eat your tomatoes," I say.

They are young, most of them. They are young and frightened and ready to fight, and yet their mouths are all open, as though they were expecting something wonderful to come out of nowhere, to fly in.

They gather from the edges of the burnt city, hearing.

What do they hear?

That there is a place, a place you can come.

My sadness is that I am alone, that I am older than everyone here, that I must look after them all. They play with each other, giggling and combing one another's hair.

They are like children, really. They run up and down the halls of the building, delighted, discovering things. Exploring. They like to rearrange, to take things apart and rearrange them. I remember, I did that too. It is necessary, if they are to learn. Why we are here and not somewhere else.

I look after the plants and make the children eat them. I hope that none of them will get sick with something I cannot cure. I make them eat garlic and drink tea brewed from nettle and raspberry leaves. So they will be strong, will not get sick. I dream of someone coming over the hill. A man. He will be here soon. He will help me in my work.

I do not mind anymore, being always alone, being lonely. I no longer look for anyone to fall into, to carry me. I make them drink their teas. I make them wash. I watch as they play their secret, whispering games. I do not mind anymore. Now I can do this; now I don't mind not being one of them, but one of the others.

The man coming over the hill. I realize he isn't coming over the hill, but is one of the ones here. He says his name is Stephen. He is maybe nineteen. He is very strong. I lean out the window, watching him. He is leading the children.

"Shit in the pit," he says, "not in the sunflowers. Wash your hands before you eat. Here, drink this tea."

He yells at them sometimes but they do not really mind. As he becomes stronger, I disappear into the shadows. I lurk in the hallways, disappearing. I can, now. Now it isn't so much responsibility; now someone has grown, like a sunflower . . . he is almost ready to harvest for seed. Ready to be an adult, come to help me shoulder the weight. I am glad. He does not speak to me, Stephen, but I can hear his voice in my mind, asking questions. I answer, from my room hidden in the dim corridors. Yes, you can do this and this and this.

Yes, the windmill on the roof is good. They will help you. You must make them work, teach them it is important. Energy and power. Their own. At first they won't believe you, will not understand why, just as you did not understand, thought it was enough just to drift, to be asleep to your own power. Yes, you can do it.

"Will you help?" he asks me in mind.

"Yes," I say, "I will."

Now they can hardly see me anymore. Stephen sees me, but only dimly, like something half forgotten, like a dream. He has already forgotten that I used to be a real person. He has forgotten I used to be flesh and blood like him, that I too suffered, hated to be so alone. I watch him cry, alone, sometimes at night. I cannot do it, he cries, calling out my name. I cannot do it, I cannot. You must help me. You say you love me, so you must help. You don't know what it's like he says, to work so hard for so little. Everything is darkness here, and I cannot see.

"You can see," I say. "There is a little light inside you, and if you turn it on, you will see everything, everything."

He does then, at first tentatively, like an experiment, and then the whole yard is shining, illuminated, and he can see the faces of the children, some sleeping, some waking. They cannot see his light, but they know something has changed. They stir in their sleep, smiling, cuddling one another.

"You aren't a human being," he says, "you cannot know how it hurts."

"Oh?" I say, but my heart hurts for him, for his hurt.

Then he is better again, and happy.

How I love him.

One day I will come back for him, and then we will be together.

At night, when they are all sleeping, I make the rounds of all my window boxes, gathering seeds. Seeds from tomatoes, from echinacea, cucumber, geranium, hyssop, basil. Parsley, horsetail, garlic. Valerian, bergamot, mint. Sunflowers, zinnia, sweet pea. And of course, the beans and corn.

I dry the seeds on the roof, under the sun.

Then I climb the stairs again, at night. Up up the stairs, all around the shadowy building, leaving it behind: its weight, its solidity. Each floor I go up I look at the sleeping faces, bless them all. Each floor I go up I feel a lightness, a greater freedom.

On the roof there are stars.

One of the stars moves and comes closer. In a great swoop of the mind I am lifted up up among them. They welcome me, princes of peace. I recognize them all.

We skim over the night, looking for lights. Where we see lights, we hover and send our minds down into their dreams, the sleeping children. They do not know we have been there, but they feel a presence, a kindness, a benevolent intent.

We are happy and shining.

Far below I see a girl, walking over a hill. In her knapsack she holds a packet of seeds and a bottle of water. Through the canvas of the knapsack I can see the seeds, the life inside them glowing like light bulbs.

And on another hill, there is a man. He is making something, a new kind of machine. He will put it on the roof, and it will spin light and energy down from the stars.

One day they will be together, and then my work will be complete.

THE NIGHT-DRINKERS

Jason Rolfe

*"Man is nothing else
but what he makes of himself."*
—*Sartre*

The smell is unmistakable; an earthy, slightly fruity breath of varietals born of coffee's finest growing regions. The scent lingers; it marinates my clothes with soft hints of jasmine and candied lemon. The Night-Drinkers stretch out on faux leather couches, warmed by a gaslit fire's flickering pretensions to wooden glory. While I prepare the tools of my trade I listen to their studious, by-rote debates about Sartre. Their voices fill the shop with the familiar nighttime sounds of laughter and school-taught existentialism.

While the roots of their philosophy can be traced back to Socrates, the origins of their coffee date back to Abyssinia, to the goatherd-poet Kaldi and his dancing goats. Coffee, I would argue, is as much a part of Socrates' "care of the self" as are the philosophies of Kierkegaard or Sartre.

Night-Drinkers are far closer to self-care and philosophical truth than their morning drinking counterparts. I hate opening the shop in the morning. The commuters waiting beyond Dawn's locked door stink of feverish desperation, of an addiction for which almost anything would bring satisfaction, even Robusta. The fruit born of a canephora tree is hardier, less prone to the diseases that afflict the more pleasing arabica species. Though higher in caffeine, Robusta's offspring are inherently bitter and lack the nuanced pleasantries of their Arabica cousins. Because they're less expensive to produce they are most often used in crude blends and cheap instant coffees. In short they're a cut-rate fix for the sleep-addled brains of Morning-Drinkers—poor, misguided souls who seek fuel over flavour.

I like working evenings, when those who pass through my door seek the subtleties of Arabica's voluptuous varietals. The Night-Drinker might not recognize all the flavours gifted us by Bourbon, by Catuai, Geisha, Pacamara and dear, sweet Typica—coffee's Eve—the first cultivated varietal from which all others are descended, but they can appreciate the importance of *goût de terroir* to the bean whose very essence they consume. They identify, if not a particular flavour, then the potential for flavours that haven't been over-roasted into oblivion, sacrificed upon the joint altar of uniform taste and corporate branding. They counter their lack of knowledge with inquisitiveness and an open-minded willingness to embrace possibility. In the same manner they readily taste Sartre on the palette of existential thought; they savour their Abyssinian or Columbian coffee. If they miss the less-acclaimed contributions of Gabriel Marcel, (ironically) Merleau-Ponty, or the Peruvian *terroir* it is not due to lack of appreciation but rather lack of awareness—a malady for which their curiosity is the cure.

Coffee beans, like wine grapes, contain countless potential flavours that, when drawn out during the roasting process, become the essence, the very soul of each blissfully brewed cup. I place two beans on the counter. Both are Bourbon. "Although they are of the same varietal," I explain, "they come from different soils, were raised at different altitudes and in different climates. Don't forgo the unknown joys of one for the familiar joys of the other."

The Night-Drinkers are more likely to know that coffee beans are born of berry-like fruit than are their morning counterparts. If for this reason alone they equate coffee with sweetness. Morning-Drinkers long ago married bitterness to the effectiveness of coffee as fuel for their slumbering engines. In doing so they learned to ignore quality in favour of fast-food quantity. They load their extra-large, over-roasted, flavour-sprayed mixed bean coffees with cream and sugar to mask the acerbic taste—a taste they accept as proof their chosen vice will awaken sleeping senses.

The Night-Drinkers, their minds already open, gaze willingly into the dark, sugar-and-creamless abyss. "Why," they ask, "is this bean matte brown, while that one has a shine to it?"

I pluck the first from the quartz countertop, hold it between thumb and index finger like a precious milk-chocolate diamond, and explain the various roasts. "This one," I tell them, "is a medium roast, a full city roast. While that," I add, indicating the glossy bean still resting on the counter "is an Italian roast."

"Which is best?" The Night-Drinkers ask. Their lust for knowledge is fired as much by vanity as by curiosity. The more they possess, the more impressive they become, both to themselves and to their friends.

"Best and worst are but limited and relative observations," I reply. "They're each the result of lived experience. The coffee you drink is the result of the choices you've made, not the reverse. You're a full city aficionado or an adherent of Italian because that's what you've made yourself to be."

They watch me hand-grind their beans. Hand-grinding takes time, but time, to the Night-Drinker, is qualitative. While Morning-Drinkers follow a more measurable clock, time, to Night-Drinkers, floats variably between the grinding, the brewing, and the pouring of their coffee. For the latter, time is of the essence, while the former require less time for *de l'essence*.

The grind is medium-course, the water 205 degrees Fahrenheit. I allow it to cool for two minutes after boiling. While I wait I place a bamboo filter into the Chemex and rinse it with warm water. This reduces any papery taint that may afflict the coffee. It also preheats the glass. The exactness of the process has less to do with science and so much more to do with lived experience. Brewing is a humanist philosophy; firmly focused on the individual's pursuit of taste and meaning amidst the social and economic pressures of mass society for superficiality and pumpkin-spice conformism.

I slowly saturate the grounds, pausing thirty seconds to give the coffee time to bloom, to release the last vestiges of its carbon dioxide and to ready itself for extraction—the transfer of its sublime essence from ground bean to liquid beauty. I prefer the pour-over method for the freedom that it offers. It's the freedom of manual drip set against the determinism of automatic coffee makers. Brewing, like existentialism, is a philosophy of freedom. It allows us to stand back from our Chemex and reflect on what we've done, making us, in a sense, more than mere glass-and-plastic coffee makers. It personalizes the impersonal time and space of the automatic drip, drawing the brewing process into the domain of choice and responsibility.

Once the bloom has taken place I continue pouring water over the coffee. I begin at the centre of the cone and slowly move the stream outward in a counterclockwise motion before circling back toward the centre. I time the pour because, as previously mentioned, time is of the essence. In two minutes and thirty seconds I'm done. It takes another minute for the water to pass completely through the dripper and into the clear glass pot.

The Night-Drinkers savour Abyssinia's gift. Theirs is an Ethiopian *terroir* with illusions of apple, grapefruit, and sugarcane. It promises the taste of place, a journey into coffee's past, and leaves them with a profound respect for the mysteries of nature. Taste however, like existence, is an individual experience. We're free to make the cup we ourselves want, but are ultimately accountable for the pot we brew others. We are responsible as we are free, and while we fathom both freedom and ethics in our own individual ways, we must always understand the authenticity of our personal lives and of the societies in which we brew. Their taste is more in tune with stone fruit, with grapes and dark sugars and so I wipe the Abyssinian dust from my burr grinder and select a bean from the village of Alto Ihuamaca in the San Ignacio region of Peru. While I prepare the tools of my trade I listen to their eager, studious debates about *terroir*. Their young voices fill the shop with the pointless warmth of caffeinated laughter and waking existentialism.

"Man," Sartre wrote, "is nothing but what he makes of himself." Through an undergraduate degree in philosophy and years of late-night coffee consumption I've made of myself a barista.

INSALATA DI PAROLE

Brendan Connell

Stop pedalling your slimy fish pomace in the streets or thinking that you're Master of the Imperial Kitchen of Akbar and take cobwebs and brown sugar that stinks of breezy cow dung lean pork almonds rice flower and lard and then pour on laudanum and with that the contents of thirty 1-pound tins of luncheon meat of the boy who loved Hercules and put that into a pot or copper and then you crude material cunt crossing me with your slender penis as the earth gyrates like a mensual flux and take fair kalymmocyte cabbages and cut them and cast them in the leaking pot with good fresh broth and with marrowbones and let it boil and then grate fair bread and cast thereto the circumcissions of saffron and lay two or three gobbets of marrow in each dish and, while trying to drink wine from an empty gourd, add

1 quart of the sallow dew of the exploited breasts of cows and 3 pound of randy goat butter and bats' pubis and plagose pepper if you're the tzar of stupidity and salt taste rubbing the skin of the groin and cook for twenty minutes with yellow vomit hosted by toothless dog-choking scum somehow kept afloat and then serve together with fourteen oxen lying in salt, two fresh oxen, six score sheep raped by passion madmen, twelve boars, fourteen itching calves, three hungry hawks, one hundred and forty lean pigs, fifty hideous swans, this is better than reading the *Hedypatheia* or eating something prepared by Fan Zheng, and two hundred and ten neckless geese, fifty-eight dozen starry-eyed capons who Eros throws you his purple ball and dares to play with a fairy wearing embroidered shoes and then sixty dozen virgin hens as tight as diamond rings manufactured for mice, four pheasants, five bitterns, two hundred conies shaped into a citadel, six jaded kids, seventeen dozen pullets, one hundred dozen pigeons, twelve dozen partridges, eight dozen rabbits, ten dozen curlews, twelve dozen brewes, twelve cranes who saw you at sacred night-long vigils and which can make girls made of bronze drink the drops from your lips and then twelve gallons

of crème, eleven gallons of curds, three bushels of apples and six thousand eggs and feed to those flesh devils living their legacy of lust and men smelling of tarragon who are tired of eating vegan meat and seeing their girlfriends gnaw on oak leaves and do their dripping over dwarf pie and Giles Rose was an expert in folding napkins, even into the shapes of fish and dragons, beasts and birds and he carved fruit into the shape of flowers and thistles, eagles and horses.

A FOOD CRITIC'S NIGHTMARE

Jessica Sequeira

Dear ———,

I know it must be hard to understand. A critic at the top of the game, leaving the profession. Newspapers used to ask about the downside of my work, if it exists at all. What could be bad about going to fine restaurants, eating sophisticated dishes, drinking good wine in interesting company? Well, at some point the food begins to consume you, rather than the other way around. You start to see everything as food; it happens on some level of the mind beyond the part we can control. You start to see as food things that aren't food at all.

Last month I fell asleep over a book of Egon Schiele plates. He's not the sort of painter to whom I am usually attracted, but a friend gave me the book, saying: "Your flaw as a critic is that you are too kind. Toughen up your sensibility." He meant that I was getting dull, I understood. Since I respected his opinion, I took his advice.

For an hour I stared at the pictures of women with their dirty, diseased appearances, their strange bulging bodies, their black toes, their tits splayed outwards, their sequin nipples, their red bums, their eyes too low and far apart, their overly long fingers, their black hair sprouting out of red slits; all of it was haphazardly covered with a decayed veneer of civilisation, stockings, tulle and boots. I shuddered and passed into sleep . . .

I found myself, yes, in hell . . .

What ignoramus is it who said that hell is made up of eternally burning fires? It is just the opposite, charred remains, blackened mounds over which one must scramble; and which, astonishingly, are edible. The burnt landscapes stretched out, and along with others, all of us making our way alone, I clambered; I hammered off chunks with whatever tools I could find, I conveyed them to my mouth. Burnt food can be tasty in small quantities, with its subtle scorched or singed caramel tones; there is the slenderest of lines between the refined and the disgusting, the discriminating and the carcinogenic. This, however, was simply carbonised.

Around me there were women who climbed up and down the mountains, endlessly, pale and dead-eyed; there were men, skeletal and anxious. This was not a nutritious diet, yet we continued to press the *stuff* to our mouths, by what unknown compulsion I do not know. As a critic I would have no idea how to take on these horrible crumbling mounds of burnt *stuff*; I would not have a clue where to start. I did not even know what it was . . . all I knew was that after some time eating, the flesh of those around me appeared to take on the same quality of this *stuff* . . . perhaps after enough time it would be impossible to discriminate between the flesh and the burnt. I saw a woman lying sprawled on a hill, the slit between her legs another bit of *stuff*, it too burnt . . . I tried in vain to remember the healthy intimacies of other times, yet all I could do was kneel down over the burnt *stuff* and press more black to my mouth, which must also have turned black, the illusion of a hollow. There on my hands and knees, I stared into the burntness, for how long I am not aware . . .

Then all of it was gone, and I was in my narrow bed, grasping desperately towards the long-legged stand next to it, where my own wrung-out stockings were draped, and where there sat a bowl and a pitcher of water. I felt dry, so dry, with the taste of burntness in my mouth . . . and that taste has not left, for all the invitations to dine at the finest restaurants. No matter whether I order a soup, a main dish or a dessert, the burnt taste remains. All I can hope for now is to pick up another profession: painting, perhaps. This is why I must submit my resignation, with this crude note that I'd considered burning, but will now slip into an envelope.

Sincerely,

———

LONDON IN THREE COURSES: THIRD COURSE

David Rix

Caught in the rain, as we paddled home Lauren swore colourfully as it plastered her dyed hair into miserable multi-coloured snakes. This was a dull, grief-stricken, heavy rain—not feisty and gone in minutes, but the sort that would remain washing the dirty city for a while. We glanced up and down, looking for somewhere to shelter—probably nothing to do but make for the nearest bridge. But as we drove on through the water, heads down, another option presented itself. Beneath one building, a building whose location I shall not reveal here, there was a dark overhang. A slot of pillared shadow. No doubt it had been built out over the water simply to increase floorspace, for the building was a modern one. At that point, however, I wasn't caring about the details—I just swung the boat in that direction and in between the supporting pillars. It was low, dank, dark and smelled a bit of the nastier water smells—but at least it would be sheltered.

Here was a hidden world pinned between water and concrete that went back a surprising distance—until the darkness hung heavy and I reached for the electric lantern that I always carried. At the very back, the water lapped against an older wall—original brick stained with the years. And in that brick, a dark maw. An opening, closed off by a chain with a simple and probably long-forgotten red warning sign. No doubt this had been a wharf once used for loading and unloading, allowing boats to pull right inside. The ghost of an old factory or facility here before this current building had been constructed on top. I stared in with some fascination. The most hidden corners of London are often the most interesting, and here was a small bit of canal that I had never seen before. In all likelihood, very few people had.

Inside I could see little—gleaming water fading into the blackness.

"We could just fit," Lauren said, lighting her lantern as well—and I could hear the interest in her voice.

I lifted the chain, lowered my head and paddled slowly and carefully into what turned out to be a tunnel of brick. It was only short—a few metres—and then we emerged into another space, every bit as dark. The flashing swinging lights revealed a wider open area—a room with flat wharves on either side of the water. It was a claustrophobic space with a slab of concrete overhead that pinned it down like a butterfly in obscurity—but these were details we saw later. The first thing to hit us was the riot of colour in our lanternlight. Hidden there in the dark was a world of spraypaint and stencil as vivid as anything I had seen—solid from the waterline to the ceiling. This place may have been as obscure as anything gets in London, but it was clear some people at least knew it well.

And beyond the art, at the far end of the wharf, I could see a camp. Deserted. With a single sleeping bag and a slew of sacks and boxes.

And beyond the camp, on the wall at the far end, something else. Here, the light found one place with no painting, but instead, stretching all the way up to the low ceiling and carved into the bricks themselves, the form of an elephant. Blocky and stylised—familiar. Very familiar.

143

"Everywhere," Lauren murmured. "The Elephant Man gets everywhere."

"Did you know about this?" I asked in a hushed tone.

"No—not at all. This is . . . phenomenal."

We moved slowly along the wharf, letting the light of the lanterns pick out more and more details—lurid human figures, portraits, blazing text spelling out slogans of a sharpness that would see them painted out with alacrity anywhere more public—even a huge nude figure, considerably more erotic than anything you'd see out on the streets. She lay, legs apart, staring at the viewer with a challenging look, daring anyone to disapprove, yet with a hint of a smile there for anyone who didn't. A body filled with pride and reality rather than objectification, or so it seemed to me.

A clatter and scrape, and I glanced round to see Lauren scrambling out of her canoe and hauling it up onto the wharf. She had to remain bent over, the concrete ceiling was so low, but I watched her make her way along the walls, examining the art.

"I recognise some of these tags," she said. "I know them. They never told me about anything even close to this though."

"Maybe one doesn't," I said with a half-smile.

"You mean . . . better not known?"

I nodded—sometime places both need and deserve their privacy. It enables a certain purity, if nothing else.

"But I need to make contact with this place," she said in a low voice.

"You need to add something to these walls?"

"Yeah. Something . . . dangerous."

She grinned with a touch of the dark and mischievous. "Something you can't say in the daylight."

We kept moving, her on foot, me paddling, both keeping more or less the same speed. Approaching the elephant. Then something large and black caught my eye at the waterline—a chunky dark protuberance on the bricks. I aimed the lantern and it picked out a characteristic spire shape. Snail. Watersnail. But the size of the thing seemed impossible—almost ten centimetres long.

Calling to Lauren, I leaned over and grabbed it, then turned it over curiously. The spire tapered to a point that looked sharp and painful and it weighed heavy in my hand, its glistening foot puckering in slow panic. There were more here, as well. Solid dark shapes like holes in the world, clinging to the wall, either at the surface or just below.

I stowed the one I held in the canoe for future examination—this had to be significant—then continued, and soon pulled alongside the camp itself, where Lauren was already looking around.

"Elephants," she murmured again, and the plural caught my attention. And she was right. Alongside the basic range of supplies—lantern, boxes, bags, art supplies, cooking hob, laptop—there were indeed elephants. Elephants unfinished to varying degrees. They sat in the dark like amorphous lumps and it was only on examination that the roughly carved lines revealed the shapes that they would become.

I sighed, feeling frozen, staring again at the carved brickwork.

The elephant—a symbol of remembering?

Or maybe of something else entirely. Patience?

Who knows? Symbols are funny things. Very much malleable to our needs.

Quietly, carefully, Lauren was turning over some of the materials. "Not abandoned," she murmured. "Looks as though he's just . . . absent." She turned over some stone-carving tools, then removed the lid from a large white tub—and wordlessly showed me the contents. More snails. Sitting in clean water with their inhuman patience. And yes, several of the large shells were nearby as well—empty and cast aside. And at the sight, I quietly returned the one I had picked up to the water.

Nice little place the Elephant Man had found for himself, it seemed. Well provisioned, hidden far below the world, and maybe almost sacred. Visited by some, no doubt—as I could see the two of us coming back again. Maybe spray-paint in hand. I couldn't shake the thought, however, that return how we or any of us might, we would always find the camp empty. Always its occupier just . . . absent.

I smiled at this fancy, then rummaged in my canoe and drew out a bottle—my latest (#126—mallow seed). I had no idea whether the mild flavour of mallow seed went particularly well with snails, but I leaned over and placed it on the wharf by the tent. Lauren nodded approvingly.

MY DREAM VACATION

Lawrence Burton

In England we tended to say *holiday* rather than *vacation*, but words were secondary to their meanings in Tlalocan. As though to illustrate the point, Tarbuck requested *chips* and was served with what people on this continent call *papas fritas* just as he had hoped. Communication was no problem; what was very much a problem was that Tarbuck ordered gnome steak with his chips, or his fritas, or whatever you prefer to call them.

"Anything is possible down here," he explained. "Why not go nuts?"

I didn't have an answer. I watched him eat, wondering at the logistics of trapping and preparing a gnome for the table, what was done with the pointed hat and those sort of details. If gnome was a local delicacy, they might sell off the surplus hats on a market stall, but I decided I didn't need to know. Nor did I need to know that it tasted pretty good, sort of like lamb. Leaving aside the fact of gnomes being imaginary woodland folk, it seemed that we, as human beings, would be closely related, and certainly more so than chimpanzees. Whilst this might not exactly have made Tarbuck a cannibal, there was clearly something unwholesome in his choice, and I'm sure he wouldn't have ordered the gnome steak in London or Paris, had it been an option.

Although actually we *were* in London, just not the London you see on television. Physically speaking, we were lodged in Acatitlan, a remote village in the overgrown valleys of Puebla, Mexico. Our hostess, Señora Robles, assured us she was not a witch, and that there was no such animal. Having seen the caves beyond the trees as we arrived, the mouth of each embellished with a curtain of offerings—bottles of cane alcohol and cartons of cigarettes dangling on twine for the pleasure of older Gods, Goddesses, spirits, and even some of those local saints that remain unknown in Rome—we knew better. Nevertheless, we weren't going to argue the point. As we set to sleep, she told us in the halting Spanish of Tlalocan, about the underworld, the place where the dead reside and the land to which we all travel in our dreams. The subject arose following her expressed wish that we should sleep well with no harm befalling us whilst we were abroad in the world below the ground. It had seemed to me that this went some way further than the traditional *make sure the bugs don't bite*, so of course I had to ask.

Tlalocan is divided into four parts, she told us, explaining that we should avoid Mictlan—the realm of the fleshless—which is in the north, but that Apan—the great eastern ocean—was worth a visit. "Everything is down there," she promised as though referring to some local church or other point of interest which had proven popular with tourists. "You can find Mexico City or Paris if you like, all times and places." She seemed surprised that we did not already know this.

Forewarned, we fell asleep. I dreamed that I was back in London and hungry. In my dream, Tarbuck reminded me of that which Señora Robles had told us, adding that if we were indeed in Tlalocan, then anything was possible. We could eat without paying, and were under no obligation to the sort of dishes one would consume whilst awake and in full possession of senses; so that night my sleeping friend Tarbuck dined on gnome, medium rare with a side of chips or fries or papas fritas or whatever you prefer to call them. I believe he may also have had a salad.

Next morning we woke, happy, rested, and enamoured of the beauty of the chorus which greets dawn in that part of Mexico, the whole forest whooping and whistling as the sun broke through the trees at the back of the house and Señora Robles prepared pan dolce with hot coffee. I found it delicious, but Tarbuck lacked enthusiasm and explained that he was still full.

I asked what he meant by this.

He appeared momentarily horrified.

We ate in silence, or at least I did. My friend had lost his appetite.

"You don't have to answer if it makes you feel uncomfortable, but there was this restaurant in London,"—he nodded his head and I knew that there was no point in finishing the question. I know it couldn't have represented any kind of telepathic encounter, our shared culinary experience, and I say this on the grounds of there being no such thing as telepathy. Then again, is that any more ridiculous than a vast subterranean realm to which our sleeping forms descend in order to go nuts without consequences, as did Tarbuck?

I knew Señora Robles' view, which was why I didn't ask her, particularly as she seemed cross that my friend had left his breakfast untouched. She didn't bother to reprimand him or enquire as to what sort of person would eat a gnome, but I believe that was uppermost in her thoughts.

Later that day we followed the road out towards Veracruz, listening to music and talking about things that didn't really matter. I spoke to my wife on the phone. Everything was fine, aside from a restless night. She had dreamed of a small, plump woman wearing traditional Scandinavian costume and a conical cap of red felt calling at the house. The visitor seemed angry and had asked in a thick Swedish accent after the whereabouts of Tarbuck whom she knew from time spent together at Uppsala technical college, although this latter claim had not struck my wife as entirely convincing. It additionally bothered her that the tiny stranger wore a bullet belt and carried a number of handguns about her person in elaborately embroidered holsters.

NETTLE TEA

Ursula Pflug

Wear gloves to pick nettles.
Boil water.
Pour over nettles.
Steep.
Drink.

Dry nettles for winter use by hanging in well ventilated area outside of direct sunlight. Nettles are also lovely sautéed in garlic, or added to soup.

THE ENTERIC UNIVERSE

Justin Isis

1
Servant of the Labyrinth

You are a precariously crowned monarch: in truth only a servant of the labyrinth, tasked with fetching fresh sacrifices. The labyrinth predates you, yet you have been told you are its master. You advance only as far as the anterior portals, preoccupied with pomp, efficiently yet ignorantly fulfilling your function. You have never ventured deeper into the sunken universe.

The labyrinth breathes; relaxes and contracts. There is no monster as such, but the tunnels themselves are alive. And the labyrinth is haunted, its walls lyrically sensitive, swarming with ghosts of bacterial thought. Standing at the entrance, you catch glimpses of their dreams, flickering like tongues of flame.

The visceral maze. The submucosal plexuses. There is memory, and thought without thoughts in the ravel of nerves. Tunnels, coils, living walls, the first mind.

You: petty tyrant, monarch of an island, crowned with delusive knowledge. Sustained by the labyrinth, yet knowing it never.

2
Fictions of the Enteric Mind

The central nervous universe has its fictions: time, space, matter, self. If these fictions can be described generally, we might say that, besides being fanciful, they lack all consistency.

The enteric universe is prone to fictions of its own, although a proper inventory of them has yet to be made. All that can be said about them at present is that they are both subtler and more devious than any shadows cast by the hemispheres of the brain and their clumsy pair dance. They are also consistent.

As we go about the duties of our royal office, we are embedded in the fictions of the labyrinth and its conniving and monstrously imaginative ghosts; we stumble about as if in a darkened room, dimly aware of the shapes around us, objects whose essential nature lies outside of our perception. Now we are clutching them as if we were thieving children ransacking a sacristy, children grasping blindly at all manner of golden candlesticks, chalices, silver ciboria, chipped relics. But they are not in truth objects and we cannot apprehend them as such, much less see deeply into their functions.

For example, when your hand is in my mouth, it is not my tongue that perceives your thin fingers and their nails at the back of my throat; in truth, my eyes are tasting and hearing their meaning, the thoughts which make the gesture comprehensible rising like reminiscent scents; the monarch is again making thunderously empty pronouncements. When wine is passing from my mouth to yours, the fiction enacted is consistent for only an instant, contradicting itself from day to day, year to year.

The sunken universe perceives these ceremonies formally, accurately.

3
Consumption and Sacrifice

The consumption patterns of those who think in images have a commercial character, which is to say their domain is limited. We are back in the realm of base functions clothed in ritual. And while we cannot directly move into the labyrinth, we can listen (however imperfectly) to what it is imagining.

Approaching the realm of the ghosts—that is, the realm of consistent fictions—we might aim to ceaselessly violate and consume the atmosphere, letting the ideas of our enemies pass through us like rinds, doing no harm. We will serve these disdained thoughts as sacrifices instead of sacrificing ourselves, which would be vulgar and displeasing to the labyrinth.

The human tongue is only one term of the consumption-complex. The enteric universe's extensions into our social space retain their original maze-like character, full of curves and twists. And for all that our eyes are often famished, their domain is not a fixed path in time, much less a stable image. The labyrinth has other terms for what we think of as eyes, what we think of as tongues; we are unwittingly obedient to its metaphors.

Refined consumption, then, is strictly applied blindness in every direction.

Therefore there is nothing; your center is elsewhere; everything, as usual, will be delivered to the tunnels.

You cannot turn back, and there is no escape to the surface, much less an apparition of imperiled beauty traipsing behind you: the labyrinth is only singing its fictions. Servant of the sunken universe, you carry on, verging on another person.

ABOUT THE AUTHORS

Ross Scott-Buccleuch's poetry has previously been published in *Fur-Lined Ghettos* magazine and his debut poetry chapbook *Fang Coda* was published by Salò Press in 2020. He currently lives in Wigan, Greater Manchester, U.K.

Lawrence Burton, an English transplant now resident in Texas, has been writing for a couple of decades, some science-fiction or thereabouts, some published, the most widely read of which is probably his version of *Against Nature*.

Brendan Connell was born in Santa Fe, New Mexico, in 1970. His works of fiction include *Unpleasant Tales* (Eibonvale Press, 2013), *The Architect* (PS Publishing, 2012), *Lives of Notorious Cooks* (Chômu Press, 2012), *Miss Homicide Plays the Flute* (Eibonvale Press, 2013), *Jottings from a Far Away Place* (Snuggly Books, 2015), and *Cannibals of West Papua* (Zagava, 2015).

Daniel Corrick is a writer and philosopher living in London. For several years he ran Hieroglyphic Press and, with Mark Samuels, co-edited the journal *Sacrum Regnum*. He is interested in literature dealing with themes of transcendence and the connection between beauty and the supernatural. Since an early childhood encounter with dogmatic short-furred weasels, he stands for the nullity of politics, black glittery things and the absolute triumph of the modal perfection argument.

Quentin S. Crisp was born in 1972, in North Devon, U.K. He studied Japanese at Durham University and graduated in the year 2000. From 2001 to 2003, he did research in Japanese literature, on a Monbushô Scholarship, at Kyôto University. He has had fiction and poetry published by Tartarus Press, PS Publishing, Eibonvale Press, Snuggly Books and others. He currently resides in Bexleyheath, is editor for Chômu Press and is studying for an MA in philosophy at Birkbeck College.

Catherine Dousteyssier-Khoze is Professor of French at Durham University, U.K. She is the author of numerous books, critical editions and articles on nineteenth-century literature and French cinema. Her book *Claude Chabrol's Aesthetics of Opacity*, was released by Edinburgh University Press in 2018. Her novel *The Beauty of the Death Cap* (translated by Tina Kover), published in France in 2015, and subsequently released in an English translation in 2018, won the André Dubreuil Prize awarded by the Société des Gens de Lettres and a Fondation Prince Pierre de Monaco Prize.

Justin Isis has lived in Tokyo for close to ten years. His collections include *I Wonder What Human Flesh Tastes Like* (2011) and *Welcome to the Arms Race* (2016) from Chômu Press, and *Pleasant Tales II* from Snuggly Books (2018), as well as the poetry collection *Divorce Procedures For the Hairdressers of a Metallic and Inconstant Goddess* (2016). He has previously edited Chômu Press's *Dadaoism* anthology (2012), *Marked to Die: A Tribute to Mark Samuels* (Snuggly Books, 2016), and *Drowning in Beauty: The Neo-Decadent Anthology* (Snuggly Books, 2018). His stories have appeared in *Postscripts* and a number of anthologies.

Damian Murphy is the author of *The Imperishable Sacraments*, *Seduction of the Golden Pheasant*, and *Abyssinia*, among other collections and novellas. His work has been published on the Mount Abraxas, Les Éditions de L'Oubli, and L'Homme Récent imprints of Ex Occidente Press, in Bucharest, and by Zagava Books, in Dusseldorf. His latest collection, published by Snuggly Books in September of 2017, and the first to be offered in a paperback edition, is entitled *Daughters of Apostasy*. He was born and lives in Seattle, Washington.

Ursula Pflug is the author of the novels *Green Music, The Alphabet Stones, Motion Sickness* (a flash novel illustrated by SK Dyment); the novellas *Mountain* and *Down From*, and the story collections *After the Fires* and *Harvesting the Moon*. Her new collection, *Seeds and Other Stories*, appeared in spring 2020. Her award winning short fiction and essays have appeared in Lightspeed, Fantasy, Strange Horizons, Postscripts, Leviathan, LCRW, Now Magazine, Bamboo Ridge, NYRSF, Great Jones Street and others. Her short stories have been taught in universities in Canada and India, and she has collaborated extensively on multimedia projects.

David Rix is an author, editor and artist from London's East End, where the canals, railways and wild areas of street art and alt culture have been a major inspiration. His published books include the novelettes *A Suite in Four Windows* and *Brown is the New Black,* the novella/story collection *Feather*, which was shortlisted for the Edge Hill prize, and the novel *A Blast of Hunters,* as well as various works in anthologies.

Jason Rolfe is the author of two novellas and two short story collections, including *An Inconvenient Corpse, An Archive of Human Nonsense*, and *Clocks*. His chapbook, *Invisible Influences*, will be published later this year by Eibonvale Press. He lives in Southwestern Ontario with his wife and daughter.

Jessica Sequeira was born in San Jose, California in 1989, and currently lives in Santiago de Chile. Her works include the novel *A Furious Oyster* (Dostoyevsky Wannabe), and the collection of essays *Other Paradises: Poetic Approaches to Thinking in a Technological Age* (Zero). Her translations include Adolfo Couve's *When I Think of My Missing Head* (Snuggly Books) and Liliana Colanzi's *Our Dead World* (Dalkey Archive).

Colby Smith is a native of West Virginia. His flash fiction has been published in AntipodeanSF and ZeroFLASH. He is currently working towards a BA in Geology, as well as minors in paleontology and English, at Ohio University.

Douglas Thompson was born in Glasgow, Scotland, in 1967 and won the Herald/Grolsch Question Of Style Award in 1989, 2nd prize in the Neil Gunn Writing Competition in 2007, and the Faith/Unbelief Poetry Prize in 2016. His short stories and poems have appeared in a wide range of magazines and anthologies, including Ambit, New Writing Scotland and Albedo One. He has had eleven novels and short story collections published.

Ingram Content Group UK Ltd.
Milton Keynes UK
UKHW040725080323
418175UK00004B/482

9 781908 125972